WRITING THE TOWN READ

Katharine E. Smith

HEDDON PUBLISHING

Fourth edition published in 2017 by Heddon Publishing.

ISBN 978-0-9932101-2-9

Cover design by Catherine Clarke

www.heddonpublishing.com

www.facebook.com/heddonpublishing

@PublishHeddon

Katharine E. Smith runs Heddon Publishing - an independent publishing house. She also works as a freelance proofreader, editor and copywriter.

She has a degree in Philosophy and a love for the written word. She works with authors all over the world and considers herself extremely privileged to do so.

A Yorkshire-woman by birth, Katharine now lives in Shropshire with her husband and their two children.

Other books by Katharine E. Smith

Looking Past
ISBN 978-0993210136

Sarah Marchley is eleven years old when her mother dies and she and her father have to learn a new way of life.
Very little changes until Sarah leaves for university and begins her first serious relationship. Along with her new boyfriend comes his mother, the indomitable Hazel Poole. Despite some misgivings, Sarah finds herself drawn into the matriarchal Poole family and discovers that gaining a mother figure in her life brings mixed blessings.

Amongst Friends
ISBN 978-0993487040

A group of three friends meet for the first time at primary school, aged four. Despite their differing backgrounds, they quickly form a strong bond, which sees them through secondary school and into the wide world beyond. Life becomes complicated when love gets in the way.
Amongst Friends turns traditional story-telling on its head, beginning with the dramatic end to the friends' story and tracing step-by-step through the twists and turns of fate and fortune.

For Chris, Laura and Edward

WRITING THE TOWN READ

PART ONE

Chapter One

The badger lies, broken, at the side of the road. Around it, the grass is moist with dew, which shines in the Cornish summer morning and creates a beautiful resting place for the dead animal.

The badger looks shocked at this sudden, cruel twist of fate. Its mouth is slightly agape, displaying sharp teeth which are no longer a threat to anyone or anything. The wide eyes stare glassily, far away into nothingness, whilst a trickle of dried blood cakes thickly into the dead animal's fur.

As a child I would have cried at this sight. My heart broke when I saw dead or injured animals. A succession of small pets did very little to harden me against the fact that animals die, and usually before their owners.

As a teenager, I would have protested loudly against the unfairness of the world. If I could, I would probably have found a way to blame my parents with those 'middle class', meat-eating ways which I was so eager to disassociate myself from.

Nowadays, I just feel a general sense of disappointment. I am no longer a child and I know it is expected of me that I just accept this kind of thing as a fact of life. It's 'just a badger'. These things happen.

This is what my boyfriend Dave would tell me. The same boyfriend who is currently standing by my car, looking at me with a raised eyebrow, swinging his bag from hand to hand.

A not-so-subtle clue that he is impatient for us to go.

My belief in animal rights got me into some trouble when I was a teenager – combined with my interest, all too predictably, in a young man. He was called Mags, lived in a caravan and was a hunt saboteur. I desperately wanted him and his friends to like me, and see I was much more than an average 16-year-old girl.

When some of the sabs went a bit too far, causing considerable damage to a hunt headquarters, and a police van, the police paid a visit to my parents, which brought them rushing up to Mags' caravan where they very embarrassingly gave me a real bollocking in front of my cool friends, and took me home.

I could hardly talk to Mum and Dad for weeks, although really I think it was a bit of a relief not to be involved in that world anymore. Eventually, my broken heart healed and I realised, with the help of my brother Russell, that Mags was a bit of an arrogant idiot anyway.

I still have the same beliefs I always did.

Hunts still make my blood boil but at last hunting with dogs is illegal and it is just good to know that I live in a country which no longer supports that so-called 'sport'.

I don't eat meat because I don't need to and I don't see why an animal should lose its life for what is essentially a few minutes' pleasure.

I still find it hard to keep my mouth shut sometimes but I understand, though find it hard to accept, that most people don't share my views. This is especially true of the rural community in which I live.

Realising that standing looking at a badger is helping nobody, I press the remote to open the car. Dave gets in to the passenger seat and I climb in behind the steering wheel, hoping that my starting the engine won't wake my neighbour Mrs Butters in the flat below mine. Normally she is up way before me, and often the gentle sounds of her kettle boiling as she potters around her kitchen listening to Radio 4 infiltrate my dreams.

Today, however, we are up ridiculously early to make sure that Dave doesn't miss his train to London. The capital city seems a whole world away from where we live, and it is amazing to me that Dave will be there before 9am. I am glad I don't have to make the journey and though I am not overly keen on such early starts, today the rising sun and the birdsong which surrounds us on all sides more than make up for it.

I open my window to feel like I am a part of this day, before turning the key in the ignition and reversing out of the drive.

Just thirty or so minutes earlier, I had been struggling to wake up. It took me a few minutes, but I was aware that the alarm clock was not going to stop beeping by itself and seemed to have made no dent whatsoever on Dave's consciousness.

I realised that, even though we were getting up at this ungodly hour for his work not mine, it would need to be me who made sure we were both awake. My whole body remonstrated with me as I stretched, and my eyes opened sorely.

I stumbled to the kitchen and leaned against the worktop as the kettle boiled, letting my body come round slowly as I stared out of the window, dimly making out the shapes of a pair of blackbirds hopping across the lawn in the burgeoning light of the July day.

Now that I am out in the world, and have glimpsed the dancing glimmer of the sunlight on the sea, I feel privileged to be up at this time.

Dave, now that he is fully awake, is lively and energetic; sure he is going to land some nice juicy work in London today.

"Are you still feeling sad about that badger?" he asks, half-teasingly.

"I am, actually," I answer, defensively, annoyed that he knew I had been thinking about it. "It's just so unfair that animals are always the ones to suffer. Just because somebody probably wanted to get home quickly. Just for the sake of convenience to humans. They don't have a choice, it's just shit."

"That's life though, Jamie. It's the way the world is. It's evolution anyway. Survival of the fittest and all that."

Dave pulls the sun visor down and smiles at himself in the mirror.

"Or perhaps that should be survival of the shittest," I say. "What kind of a world is it where only the most selfish survive?"

"That would be this world, my dear, and it may not be fair but like I say, that's life."

We've had this discussion, or variations of it, so many times. I can't say I'm totally comfortable with it as it reminds me how differently Dave and I think on certain things but then Dave is a different person to me. Maybe I've just clung on to my teenage views too long. I can't just sit back though, and accept there's nothing we can do about the things that we think are wrong in the world.

That said, I do actually find the carefree side of Dave attractive. He has an easy air about him, and doesn't get too bogged down in worries. It's good for me sometimes as it makes me stop to wonder if I am worrying about nothing. Dave doesn't waste his time worrying. He just gets on with life.

While I sometimes find it hard to sleep at night, with worries somehow magnifying in the dark, Dave falls asleep almost instantly and, as far as I can tell, sleeps all the way through the night, his mouth puckered open and his forehead smooth and relaxed.

Despite all our differences, I would not want to change Dave. I never thought I would fall so easily into a relationship. My friends and family were as shocked as I was but somehow Dave just felt right. I know that sounds cheesy but it's true. I can hardly believe we haven't even known each other a year and I can't imagine life now without him.

"Do you know what time you'll be back tomorrow? Do you want me to pick you up?"

"I don't know. If it's late I'll get a cab, no point in you waiting up for me."

"Well let me know if you do want a lift; it'll save you the cab fare and I'm not planning to do anything."

"Thank you, my loverrr."

Dave, Manchester born and bred, finds it highly amusing to try and imitate the West Country accent. Needless to say, his attempts at mimicry are rubbish.

Secretly, I am quite pleased at the thought of a night in on my own. I can watch whatever I want on TV, or perhaps just sit and read all night. I do like to have some time to myself and although I love Dave living with me, I sometimes miss the freedom of living alone.

I should really give Mel a call too; I haven't spoken to her since the weekend. I am wary of forgetting my friends just because I'm in a relationship. Not that I could ever forget Mel.

"It could be quite exciting today," Dave says, "Now that we, or should I say *London*, has got the Olympics; there should be loads of work coming out of that. I need to get around all the agencies today. Early bird catches the worm. A rolling stone gathers no moss. A stitch in time saves nine. This time next year we could be millionaires."

"You are *such* a dickhead," I grin.

The day is warming up already and the fresh smell of the recently-cut hedgerows mixes with the subtle saltiness of the sea air. Over the fields, I can see swallows and housemartins darting and swooping like fighter planes, catching bugs. Since living in Bristol,

I have come to realise how much I'd previously taken all of this for granted.

I feel so lucky right now; in the middle of my favourite season, in my favourite place in the world. Even though midsummer is now passed, and we are officially heading towards autumn, there is still so much of summer to enjoy and the next few weeks hold the promise of long, lazy, hazy days by the sea.

At the station, Dave gives me a hurried kiss on the mouth, grabs his bags from the back seat, and is gone. I watch him walk through the doors before I turn the car around and head back towards the coast.

If I'm lucky, I'll have time for a leisurely breakfast in my garden before I have to be at work. Turning the radio up, I listen to the delight over London winning the bid for the 2012 Olympics and think what a good time it is to be in this country.

Dave assessed the time and the Departures board, making the executive decision to attempt a fare-jump.

There was not enough time to buy a coffee and a ticket, and he was sorry but at this time of the morning, coffee had to come first. If he had to he could pay on the train and use the old hard-working-man-nearly-missing-the-train excuse.

He waited in the queue in the coffee shop, alternately checking his watch and eyeing the cute girl who was serving drinks. She knew he was watching him, he could tell, and when his turn came he offered her his most winning smile while he asked for a latte and croissant. She returned his smile shyly, and hurried to the coffee machine. She charged him for the coffee only, smiling meaningfully as she did so. Dave winked at her as he thanked her, then walked to the platform, smiling inside. He'd always enjoyed flirting; he knew he was good at it and it never hurt to be reminded that he was still attractive to girls other than his girlfriend.

Chapter Two

I avoid the badger's gaze guiltily when I get home, turning away from it and letting myself into the flat.

I can hear Mrs Butters' radio as I make my way upstairs. She is 'getting on a bit', as she says herself, and has the radio on pretty loud as her hearing 'isn't what it used to be'.

I bought this flat not long after returning to Cornwall. At the time, I had been staying at my parents' house and looking for somewhere to rent.

I was sitting by the window in a café, trawling the small ads and enjoying a quiet coffee and the sea view, when I felt a jab in my back. I turned to see an old lady with an impressive head of brown hair glaring at me from over my shoulder.

"Didn't you hear me?" she said angrily.

"Erm, no, sorry, I didn't," I said, flustered and wondering what I had done wrong.

"I said, *excuse* me, I need to get past and I can't get my trolley past you. If you hadn't taken a table far too big for you, there would have been plenty of space."

"Alright, alright, keep your hair on!" I muttered to myself, standing up to let her past.

"I *beg* your pardon!"

Evidently I had not muttered as quietly as I'd meant to. She pushed past me and in doing so made me knock my coffee, spilling it into its saucer. I watched, red-faced, as she marched outside, dragging her tartan trolley behind her.

I turned to the only other customer to shrug my shoulders, trying to hide my embarrassment, only to see another old lady hiding behind a menu, her shoulders shaking with silent laughter.

"I'm sorry," she said, "I'm not laughing at you. You've just made my day, that's all. Denise is so proud of that new wig."

"It's a wig?" I said, feeling my face colour even more.

"Oh yes, but don't worry dear, it's purely for vanity's sake.

Anyway, she was being unforgivably rude to you. Sorry, I should have told her off but I thought you might not appreciate me sticking my nose in. Then you made me laugh so much. Can I buy you a replacement coffee?"

She joined me at my table and I introduced myself.

"Edna Butters," she said, with a friendly smile. *Mrs Butters*, I thought; what a nice, comfortable name.

When she clocked that I was looking at ads for renting, Mrs Butters (I somehow have never been able to call her Edna, even though she tells me to time after time) said she had a proposition. She was having her house made into two apartments, enabling her to stay in her home whilst freeing up some money to pay for her medical care. Would I be interested in buying the upstairs flat?

I could hardly believe my luck, and I still marvel at the way such a minor incident provoked such a great twist of fate in my life. Now I have a flat with a 'sea glimpse', as one of the tourist brochures would say, and a garden of my own too. I have reaped the benefits of the hard work Mrs Butters and her late husband Alfred put into their garden; all their careful planning and planting.

Dad put down some decking for me which is just big enough for a table and two chairs. If both my parents come around, I usually end up sitting on the lawn looking up at them, feeling a bit like a child again.

Just as I sit down with my breakfast, I hear Mrs Butters' back door creak open, so I pop my head over the fence to say hello.

"Hi Jamie, dear," she calls, waving a gloved hand which is brandishing a trowel.

"I can't believe you're out here working already!" I say.

I wish her an enjoyable day then return to my breakfast and book. The gulls are screeching away above me, preparing for another happy day stealing pasties and chips from the tourists.

I take a deep gulp of the strong coffee I've made in an attempt to convince myself I'm not really tired. When Dave's here I tend to stay in bed with him, enjoying the companionable moments of warmth until I absolutely have to get up. Consequently I haven't sat outside at this time of day for ages.

All too soon, it's time to get to work. I walk as quickly as I can down the lane and through town to the *Advertiser* offices, thinking jealous thoughts about the holiday makers who will be enjoying 'my' town while I sit at a computer. I shouldn't feel jealous, I know; at the end of this week or the next they will be travelling back upcountry, to their jobs and their landlocked homes, whereas I will still be here by the sea.

I just hope the weather stays this good for the weekend.

I get into the office to see the editor of the paper, Guy Wise (yes, really) perched on the edge of my desk. My heart sinks.

Guy is like a caricature, and if he has ever seen *The Office*, I can only think he believes that it is a real documentary and that David Brent is an excellent role model.

He is very keen on mixing his business metaphors, "Let's hit the ground running with this hot potato," being a direct quote, and is of the 'work hard, play hard' school of thought. We have been ordered more than once to attend work social events and told threateningly that we must enjoy them.

The sexist attitudes which sadly prevail in workplaces around the country are only encouraged by him.

As an illustration, an average *Advertiser* staff meeting may contain the following, or similar:

1.   Three mentions of how attractive Madeleine, a student who works for us during university vacations, is.

2.   Two mentions of lapdancing clubs, usually accompanied by some kind of snorting laughter from Guy.

3.   One direct comment to Sheila, my friend and colleague, regarding how big her breasts are. Yes that's right, actually to her face. Unbelievable.

4.   A few throwaway comments about 'the wife' and credit card bills from endless shoe and handbag shopping. Ha ha ha. Women, eh?

5.   Commentary on the attractiveness (or otherwise) of some 'bird' from the TV, or any female visitor who has been lucky enough to spend some time in our office.

6.   At least one hilarious quip about how women belong in the kitchen.

As you can tell, it is very funny working in this office.

When I first started work here I tried to protest in a light-hearted way, about the way women were discussed in the office, but predictably my 'radical' view was just laughed at.

Sheila, who has worked at the paper five years longer than me, tells me to take it in my stride and laugh it off, but I'm afraid I find that too difficult. And, love Sheila as I do, I can't help but think she's made a rod for her own back by laughing along with 'the boys' (who, I might add, are very far from boyish, the youngest being 43).

At least nobody has ever made comments directly to me as they do towards Sheila. I think it is fairly clear that they would be extremely unwelcome.

I suppose things have changed to some extent because here are Sheila and I, both female reporters on the local paper of the town I grew up in. Sheila was actually the first female reporter to work for the *Advertiser*.

I've come to think that the best thing I can do is tell Guy to shut up when he goes too far, and to crack on with my job. My hope is that by being the best at what I do, I can be successful in my career, not hampered by my gender, and I might also be able to get people to see things a bit differently through what I write.

This is not easy when the majority of my work tends to be stories about the new intake of four-year-olds at the local school (complete with obligatory 'cute kids' picture) or the annual fruit and veg show.

I have definitely learned a lot more about people since I have had to work for a living and a lot more about the prejudices out there. Thankfully I have enough good men in my life to remind me they are not all sexist idiots. My brother, who is away travelling at the moment, my dad, and of course, my lovely boyfriend. Dave is fully supportive of what I do, and never minds me working long hours. At home, I do the cooking and he washes the dishes. Neither of us cleans more than we have to but the cleaning we don't do is in equal measures.

In the meantime, I just need to keep plugging away and refusing to accept things in the way that Sheila does. It takes a long, long time for things to change but I've learned to be hopeful that maybe one day there will no longer be a need for feminism to exist.

"Morning, Guy!" I smile brightly at my boss, trying to convince us both that I like him.

"Just made it before we locked the gates, eh Jamie?" he smiles back at me. I will say this for him - he's not a complete control freak and will tolerate a little lateness or slightly longer-than-usual lunch breaks from any of his staff, as long as we don't make a habit of it.

Also, he is to some extent in my good books at the moment as I am currently being entrusted with a big story - researching and reporting on the problem of a gang of teenagers which has become progressively more prevalent in town life over the last year or so. It has become a matter of real concern as people here have never really experienced anything like this before.

Having lived for some years in Bristol, I'm aware that far worse happens in bigger cities, but that doesn't make it any more acceptable.

Luckily, as this is such a small place, it does mean that it's difficult, if not impossible, to keep most things truly a secret. This includes the identity of the trouble-makers. There have been a number of rumours as to whether they are our 'own' kids or from out of town. Sooner or later I am sure they will trip themselves up and I know there are a good number of local blokes just waiting for the chance to sort them out.

Not that I am in favour of vigilante-type crime fighting, but I do think that these kids need to be scared by people they might, or at least should, have some respect for.

The incidents started with some minor vandalism in the town gardens and along the sea front. Lately, however, the malevolent nature of the gang's behaviour has escalated. A couple of younger boys have been bullied and a local man was mugged on his way back from the pub one night.

I try to be sympathetic towards people, and understand their behaviour. I don't believe people are inherently 'bad' and I am sympathetic to the viewpoint that the kids in this gang are perhaps from a deprived background, uncaring families, that kind of thing.

Also, as I mentioned, I got into a little bit of trouble myself as a teenager. Although at the time I would swear blind that what I did was to further the cause of animal rights, I now see it was also born from the desire to impress, and the general frustrations of being a teenager.

Whereas I was from a relatively privileged background, there are many people here who are not. Despite this town being a hugely popular tourist destination, for the teenagers who live here, if they are not very well off, there is actually not a great deal to do.

However, this in no way excuses the gang's behaviour,

particularly when it comes to personal attacks upon individuals; there is no way I could begin to justify or understand this level of nastiness.

I have been able to speak to the guy who was mugged at the weekend and I think that the kids who did it may just find they messed with the wrong person. As I tell Guy, "He says he was a bit the worse for wear from drinking but he managed to land a punch on one of them and he's sure he knows who it was. I guess a black eye would be a bit of a giveaway."

"Don't suppose he gave you a name?"

Guy looks hopeful – it would be a bit of a coup to be able to say the *Advertiser* helped to solve the problem.

"No, he won't, and he says he won't tell the police either. I'm wondering whether he is thinking of sorting this out himself; he did seem to be making some fairly thinly veiled threats. I hate what's going on, you know I do, but as a news story it's quite an exciting thing to be writing about. I'd like to really make something of this story, Guy."

I am aware I am smiling at him rather ingratiatingly and hate myself for it, but it seems to work.

"Fine," Guy says, "As long as you keep me up-to-date and do your share of the bread-and-butter stories too."

"Like covering the fruit and veg contest? Wild horses wouldn't keep me away."

Guy snorts.

I walk away, feeling pleased, and slightly warmer towards Guy. This happens from time to time. I'm just so pleased Guy is letting me take this story, when there are older, more experienced (male) reporters like Brian or Jerry, who he could have given it to.

Guy is a nightmare, no doubt about it; an ex-Londoner who's worked on local magazines and papers all his life. He moved to Cornwall with his second (predictably, much younger) wife and young family, leaving the first lot in London and complaining regularly and incredibly inappropriately about his ex-wife and the child maintenance he has to stump up.

Guy also subscribes to that strange custom of local papers, adding slightly odd one-word sub headings to articles. I think the traditional method is to take a pin, stick it in an article and use whichever word it lands in.

Still, to give Guy his due, he's happy to let us go after stories ourselves as long as we run them past him. He can even be good at giving praise.

I almost feel something akin to fondness for him as I think about this. I turn back to look at him. He is grinning at his computer screen, which is displaying a large picture of a pair of naked breasts. He snorts with laughter.

I think better of this crazy 'fondness' notion. The man's clearly an idiot.

Vegetable & Flower Entries Invited

Gardening enthusiasts throughout the area are being invited to enter this year's Vegetable & Flower Show.

The event, scheduled for the 18th September, has almost 100 different awards to offer, based on six different categories, including 'Flowers' and 'Vegetables'.

Vegetable

Fred Hutchinson, who has taken gold position in a number of vegetable categories over the years, says that the sunshine we've enjoyed this summer promises to make this show one to remember. Fred has been top of the pops in the Open Onion Championship for the last eight years. That's shallot of onions! Do you think you've got what it takes to beat him?

Pansy

Doris Stapleton has been participating in the show since it first began nearly thirty years ago and last year was finally able to claim first prize in the Perfect Pansies category. She told the Advertiser that she welcomed any newcomers and potential competition, to keep her on her toes.

Even if you're not a gardener yourself, the show promises to be a great day out, with children's games, a bouncy castle, tombola and of course Cornish Cream Teas in the Refreshment Tent.

Once on the train, Dave kept an eye out for the conductor and made a swift exit to the toilet, where he stayed until he was sure he must be safe. He reclaimed his seat and sat back, sipping his coffee and thinking about work, re-planning his itinerary of visits to possible employers, and thinking about his love life.

Jamie was lovely, there was no doubt about it, but after a few months of the quiet life, Dave had started to feel a little uneasy. Was he missing out on something else, something better?

Of all the girlfriends he had ever had, he definitely liked her best. She was so easy-going compared to her predecessors. She didn't take hours to get ready if they were going out, she wasn't into shopping. Contrary to his usual preferences, she didn't have iron-straight blonde hair and had never been on a sunbed in her life. OK, perhaps she wasn't as immediately, obviously attractive as those who had gone before, but he had to admit he was really fond of her.

Of course he knew better than to use the word 'fond' with her. He had learned the hard way that girls just didn't seem to take his being 'fond' of them as much of a compliment.

Perhaps it was the living together; he should really have got a place of his own but somehow it had never really become an issue and as Jamie had never pushed it, why should he? She was out all day at work and he was able to get on with his own projects in peace, then she would come home and they'd cook their dinner together. He'd never imagined himself being the domestic type but somehow, he couldn't deny, it worked with her.

Equally though, he couldn't deny how excited he was about going to London.

Much as he liked Cornwall, there was the unshakeable sense of purpose in a big city. Whereas Jamie would criticise the way people in a city like London were selfish and unfriendly, he knew it was because they were just intent on what they had to do. Driven, motivated people, who inspired him to be like them.

See how it goes, he told himself. Who knew what he might get out of his meetings today? Maybe he should just try and get away a bit more, up to London, Bristol, Manchester, and make the most of both worlds.

Dave glanced up to check his bag was safely installed in the luggage rack then closed his eyes, intending to doze; glad that he was not at a table so that nobody was sitting opposite to see if he dribbled.

He woke up only as the train was drawing into Paddington. Unbelievably, it was even earlier than scheduled. That had to bode well.

Dave pulled the Underground map from his pocket, re-checking his route to get to King's Cross. He had planned this day meticulously, his meetings carefully scheduled, allowing for possible delays on the Tube. He'd learned from previous experience that turning up red-faced and sweaty, with minutes to spare, was not the best way to feel confident and at ease. Today was going to be a hot one as well.

Even in winter he found the Underground stifling, so he wasn't particularly looking forward to getting crushed into somebody's armpit during the rush hour. He'd opted for a white shirt; cooler and less likely to show up sweat than a more colourful choice, but he knew that in a few hours the cuffs and collar would be looking grubby from the London dirt that just couldn't be escaped.

One mark to Cornwall, he thought – you don't get black snot in that clear, salty air. He found that despite his earlier thoughts, he was actually looking forward to going back there tomorrow. He would make the most of his night away though of course.

Dave checked through his bag, confirming he had his laptop, his notebook, his client references. As a matter of course he checked he had his building society book and his passport too (well you never knew what opportunities might present themselves... plus he hadn't really told Jamie about his savings yet so best to keep all evidence safe). All in place.

He had given a lot of thought to his meetings and was confident he'd be getting at least a couple of jobs. Today was going to be a good day.

Cornwall seemed a world away; hard to believe he had been there just a matter of hours ago. Opening his eyes wide to convince himself he was wide awake, he hurried towards the Underground station and bought a travel card from one of the machines. First stop, King's Cross.

Chapter Three

About half an hour after I have arrived at work, Guy calls me into his office.

"I need you to go out this morning, Jamie; up to Oakdale Farm. You know Bernard's been a good supporter of ours and he's asked for some publicity for this Open Day they're planning."

I know Oakdale Farm; Bernard Cooper is the father of my brother Russell's best friend, Simon. Guy loves Bernard not just because he regularly takes up advertising space in the paper, but also because he is (secretly) the 'Grumpy Old Man' from the annoying whingey column that I wish would be taken out of the paper. It's usually full of complaining about these crazy New Age people – you know the type, those who actually care about the environment or who might, Heaven forbid, be *vegetarian*.

The Grumpy Old Man column is real 'you don't understand our country ways' bullshit. Having said this though, I do like Bernard and I know he hams it up when he's writing.

To be honest, I would rather stay in the office and get stuck into my research on the gang storyline, but as it's a lovely day, the prospect of going to Oakdale is quite an appealing distraction. The views from the farm are incredible, stretching across the moors and over the sea.

"Do I get a photographer today?" I ask. We only have Dan at the moment, Sheila's husband, who can only do some part-time work for us.

"Sorry, no, you're going to have to do it yourself."

I knew this was the case really; I just like winding Guy up about it as it was his fault we lost Tony, our previous photographer. Guy just pissed him off one too many times and consequently Tony walked out earlier this year. He is now selling prints of his photos to tourists and doing pretty well out of it. We haven't been able to find a replacement at the *Advertiser* yet.

As I walk out of the office, I am aware that Guy is following me, just a shade too close as normal. I quicken my pace, then jump as Guy claps his hands together loudly.

This is his usual trick to make everybody stop what they're doing and look at him. Bear in mind that this office is really only a few square metres in size so doesn't exactly warrant hand-clapping to get everyone's attention. A gentle clearing of the throat would suffice.

"Everybody," he says loudly, "Jim's coming in to see me this morning and he wants a meeting with us all at half one so make sure that whatever you're doing this morning, you're back here on time."

'Jim' is Jim McKay, a senior manager from Avalon, the company which owns our paper and most of the others around the South West. Guy predictably sucks up to him whenever he's around, but Jim never appears to be particularly impressed. It's unusual for him to visit us at such late notice, but I don't suppose it's anything very exciting. I look at Sheila to see if she knows anything – Guy sometimes treats her as a confidante. She just shrugs her shoulders.

"Right, back to work, people."

Another clap of the hands from Guy, to banish us back to our jobs. He's like a sweaty pantomime genie.

I borrow Guy's car to get up to the farm, and have to dust crisp crumbs off the front seat. Using a tissue, I wipe the slightly greasy paw prints from the steering wheel and gearstick.

Soon out of town, I have to close the windows as the sea wind, unobstructed by buildings, is much stronger here and is blowing my hair all over my face. The car soon heats up and I can feel my cheeks starting to turn pink as I reach the farm.

As I pull into the farmyard, I'm greeted by a very friendly border collie, all wagging tail and lolling tongue. We got our family dog, Sam, from Oakdale, so this is probably one of his relations. I crouch down to be greeted by a lot of licking and excited whining as the dog seems unable to control its excitement at receiving a visitor.

"Ruby! Leave Jamie alone!"

I look up and see Simon crossing the yard, wearing a t-shirt which says 'I'm with stupid' and has an arrow pointing up at his face. I smile.

"Hi Simon, how are you?"

"I'm good thanks Jamie, nice to see you," Simon kisses me on the cheek, "Sorry you're stuck with me today, Dad's not at his best. He says hello, though."

Bernard has been suffering from ill health for some time now, which is the main reason Simon came back to Cornwall. He had been living and working in London until a year ago, working in software development. I wonder whether he minds returning to farming; does it feel like a step back or a return home?

"Say hello to him from me. I hope he's feeling better soon," I tell Simon, "And sorry but I haven't got loads of time this morning; we've got some meeting or other at the office later on."

We chat about Russell and his adventures abroad as we walk over to the pig houses. I can't help but notice Simon looks so much healthier than he did when he used to come back home for visits from his IT job.

I follow him into one of the outbuildings where he shows off a new litter of piglets. There are six tiny pigs, suckling from their mother. He grabs one and I now understand the meaning of 'ear splitting', as the tiny animal squeals and shrieks in indignation. The mother looks up and grunts, annoyed but seeming to trust Simon. The other piglets are disturbed momentarily but are soon sucking greedily again.

Simon talks gently to the piglet until it seems to calm down, and I take a few shots of the two of them. He then carefully places it back with its brothers and sisters.

I can never understand this; the level of care given to these animals and yet they are going to be sausages, bacon, pork. Killed, chopped up and sold on, to make money.

I can't afford to think like this while I'm working though and instead ask him about the Open Day, which is the reason I'm here, after all.

We walk through the farmyard and out onto the open land behind the barns. The wind hits us hard. My breath is taken momentarily not just by the strong gusts but also those views.

I struggle to hear all of Simon's words as he walks ahead of me but I can't help stopping just for a moment to take it all in. There are white-tops on the sea today, and the clouds are moving fast above us, casting shadows which sweep over the water, across the moors, and out of sight.

There is a neatly-mown field set by for the Open Day, and Simon tells me about the stalls they will have here, as well as the working sheepdog and birds of prey displays. Not to mention the obligatory hog roast. Simon grins at me when he tells me that.

"And what are the vegetarian options?" I ask, knowing that veggie food is not even considered at the country fairs and fêtes we have around here.

"Actually Jamie, we're doing some veggie cheese and apple sausages."

I consider myself corrected, but I still don't think I'll be coming. I tend to avoid these things because of their link to the meat trade; is that ridiculous of me? It's not really Dave's type of thing anyway.

I am looking forward to a trip to a quiet cove, for a picnic and a swim in the sea. The town's beaches are beautiful but at this time of year they are packed out so we prefer to have our beach days elsewhere.

I take more photos of the farm and make sure I've got all the details from Simon.

I have to push Ruby out of the car when I'm leaving, as she seems to think she's coming with me. As I drive off into the openness of the moors, I look in my rear view mirror and I can see her little black and white figure watching my departure forlornly from the dusty farmyard.

When I look back again she has gone, replaced by a thin could of dust which twinkles in the sunlight.

Back at the office, Guy is engrossed in a phone conversation. I can hear his guffaw as I walk through the door. Through the glass partition to his office, I see him reclining, feet on desk, in the big leather swivel chair which takes up a disproportionate amount of space.

I set my bag down and switch on my computer. I estimate maybe an hour to write up the Open Day story; I may as well do it now so it's out of the way. I wonder if I will ever get on in the world of journalism when all I have in my portfolio is this kind of story. Surely it must be down to the quality of the writing as well. I hope. I am really looking forward to getting stuck into the gang storyline.

Provincial it may be, but I am really quite excited by my first chance to write about something relatively big.

Open Day at Simon's Farm!

Local lad Simon Cooper is seen here with a new-born piglet, one of the stars of this coming Saturday's Open Day at Oakdale Farm, which is a chance for all to learn about life on the farm and sample some genuine Cornish Cream Teas!

Local residents and visitors to the town are all invited to come along and enjoy the day.

Simon returned to work on his family farm last year when his father, Bernard, well-known around town for his work with the Rotary Club, fell ill.

Birth

Simon told the Advertiser, "While I miss London in some ways, it is great to be back and I do not miss office life at all. The early mornings are hard work but it's so rewarding, especially when I get to help birth the animals.

"This is an extension of our open door policy as we welcome visits from schoolchildren, students and anybody with an interest in farming life."

In the evening Simon and his friends will be serving local cider and beer, and there will be a hog roast whilst Penzance band The Airjets will be providing entertainment.

Dave was in luck, and jumped onto a train on the Hammersmith & City Line which would take him straight there. He'd arranged his first meeting of the day with Sam Walters. Sam was Managing Director of a graphic design agency and they had worked together before.

Stopping for a cigarette outside the station, Dave looked around, marvelling at the sheer number of people: business men and women talking intently into their mobile phones; tourists looking keenly around, checking maps. A group of school children with two harassed-looking teachers; a pair of glamorous women with expensive-looking sunglasses pushed back over equally expensive-looking haircuts.

People of all ages and so many different nationalities. Dave was keenly aware that he had hardly seen a black person in months; Cornwall was hardly a cultural melting pot.

He felt a buzzing in his pocket – a text from Sam:

Hi 1 of kidz ill I need to find childminder. Will call u later, soz. S.

Cursing inwardly; he'd got up practically in the middle of the night for this, and now had nearly three hours to kill before his next meeting, Dave finished his cigarette and crushed its remains beneath his smart brown work shoes. He turned straight back into the station; perhaps he would hop on a train to Leicester Square and have a little meander around. Maybe get a paper and sit out in the sunshine, indulge in a bit of people-watching.

He was in two minds as to whether to take the first train that came, it was so crowded. Looking at all the people hurrying onto the platform though, it was clear that it wasn't going to get any less busy for some time yet. He squeezed his way on just before the doors closed and tucked his bag under his arm; its presence there made him feel confident and secure. Having had his luggage stolen on a previous train journey, he now always felt the need to know exactly where his bag was. He reached for the handrail, surreptitiously eyeing his fellow passengers without making eye contact.

So wrapped up in his thoughts and plans was Dave that the hand which slipped its way expertly into his bag never even registered with him. Riding the Tube was an intense experience when fresh out of Cornwall – so many people and faces, so much unwanted bodily contact with strangers.

All of this also made it the perfect place for picking pockets.

The train rushed along, and in the warm, humid atmosphere, Dave's sleepy body quickly became used to the steady, rocking rhythm. He rolled his shoulders back a little, to relax them.

BOOM.

The carriage flashed white.

The world turned black.

Chapter Four

I am uploading the pictures I got at Oakdale when Brian comes rushing in and switches on the radio.

"Have you heard?" he asks, looking flustered, and I look at him calmly, well-used to Brian's over-dramatic ways. He came rushing into the office in an identical manner when he had heard that the town was due to get its own Argos store.

"What is it, Brian?"

"Well, it's, I'm not sure, it's… listen…"

Brian fiddles about with the radio. I mentally roll my eyes heavenwards and return to my pictures until he gets it tuned in and what I hear tears my attention fully away from my screen.

"News is coming in of an incident on the London Underground or, very possibly, several incidents. There have been reports of several explosions on the Underground, affecting six trains and bringing the network to a standstill. These are yet to be confirmed by the authorities; rest assured we will keep you up-to-date with the latest news."

I look at Brian, taking a moment or two to register what's just been said. This sounds like something major. I think immediately of Dave. I can't believe he has gone to London today. I hope he's OK. I reach instinctively for my mobile and dial his number. It's probably nothing, he'll probably laugh at me, but it will put my mind at rest and perhaps he knows more about what's actually going on. I do work for a newspaper after all, and although it's only a local paper we do sometimes include a snippet of news from The World Outside.

Nothing happens for a long time, and then just a long, high-pitched '*eeeeeeeeeeeeeeeeeeee*' sound.

I try again but the same thing happens. My heart's beating faster now, even though I know it's stupid to be worrying. There's nothing even confirmed yet about the 'incidents', although something must have happened. The cautious nature of the radio reports suggests that this is really something to worry about.

Still, in a city the size of London, what were the chances that Dave would have been anywhere near whatever is going on? But then why can't I get hold of him?

I don't say anything to Brian, who has turned the radio up and is staring at it as though he can see the words coming through the speakers before they reach his ears.

"We're getting more reports of the same, although we are still waiting for confirmation from the London authorities of the nature of these incidents. There have also been reports that the problem is actually due to a huge power surge. What is clear is that the London transport system seems to have been brought to an abrupt halt, tubes and roads alike. Keep tuned in for the news as it comes in.

We've heard from several sources that there have been explosions on six tube trains and on a London bus. No more details are known as yet. If you're thinking of travelling into London though, you would be well-advised to make alternative plans. The whole of the city is apparently at a standstill."

At this point, Sheila comes in from the street with her camera slung over her shoulder, closely followed by Jerry.

"What's going on?"

"Listen to this," says Brian, "Something's going on in London, some explosions, they don't know what's happened yet. This sounds bad though."

"London? Isn't Dave in London today?"

Sheila looks as though she regrets this question as soon as she looks at me. I can understand what people mean when they say their heart is in their mouth.

"Have you called him?" asks Sheila, determinedly light-hearted.

"I can't get through. No ring tone, no voicemail, no nothing."

"Well, look, don't worry. That doesn't mean anything. Perhaps he's on the Tube."

"That's where the explosions were."

"Oh."

We all look in unison at the radio, not knowing what to say. I don't really believe that Dave will have been caught up in this, but whether he was or not, this sounds really, truly scary.

Guy chooses this moment to burst out of his office, looking very pleased with himself.

"Hi gang, looking forward to the meeting? It's going to be a big 'un. Like mine. Ha ha ha. What's up?"

Even Guy, possibly the most obtuse individual I have ever met, can't fail to notice that something isn't quite right.

"Something's going on in London," says Jerry.

"London?" asks Guy and it occurs to me that many of his family live in London, including his ex-wife and their children.

"What kind of 'something'?" asks Guy, looking around at us all.

"Something's happened on the Tube," I tell him, "They think it might be a power surge."

"Or it might have been explosions," Brian adds, helpfully.

"How can they not know? What trains? Is it terrorists?"

"I don't know," I say, not able to get Dave out of my head, "Let's just listen to this. Or could we get the TV from your office please Guy?"

"Well, seeing as it's a special occasion, I suppose so."

Guy looks a bit grey in the face, despite his attempt at levity. He gets his mobile out of his pocket, presses a couple of buttons and holds it to his ear.

"Dammit," he mutters, and tries again and again. I guess he's phoning his kids.

"Can't get through, it's not even going to voicemail."

"I had the same problem when I was trying Dave," I tell him.

"Dave? Why are you calling him?"

"He's gone to London today," I say and look at him. It's like a moment of understanding, which is a rare thing with Guy. We're both thinking the same thoughts about our loved ones. Even though there are millions of people in London and Dave is probably safely installed in his meeting, Guy's kids in their classrooms, it's impossible to relax until we actually speak to them. Hear from their own mouths that they're OK.

"Don't worry, you two," says Sheila, "There must be loads of people trying to call London, maybe they're having network problems?"

I plug in the TV and switch on BBC1, fiddling with the aerial until we get a clear reception. They've gone to constant news coverage which is not a great sign. We all gather around the screen. There are conflicting reports about explosions, power surges, one bus, three buses... Nobody seems to know much but there is an urgency and weight to this that makes my stomach churn.

I'm reminded of being at work in Bristol when the planes hit the World Trade Centre. Again that was announced by the office drama queen and I just didn't get it, I couldn't contemplate the severity of the situation, until I saw the gut-wrenching footage for myself.

A kind of awed hush falls as we stare intently at the television, confused but determined to try to make sense of the situation.

Guy and I keep trying our phones but to no avail.

"I bet it's bloody Al Qa'eda," says Guy, "Bastards."

"We don't know that," says Jerry, "In fact we don't know anything."

On the television, the presenter tells us that mobile phone networks have indeed gone down, due to a sudden unexpected demand. This is a bit of a relief and I tell myself to stop worrying about Dave. I'll catch up with him later. For now I want to know what on earth is happening. Guy also looks a little easier, although with so many friends and family living in London he must still be scared.

Guy's office phone rings. He hesitates, not wanting to take his eyes from the screen, but reluctantly goes to answer it.

"Guy Wise... Oh hi, hi Jim. Yes, yes, I've heard, isn't it terrible? Is she really? Have you managed to talk to her? Well one of the girls here is terribly worried, trying to contact her boyfriend, but I've reassured her that the networks are probably down."

Even in this situation Guy can't help but try to impress Jim. And what is it with calling us 'girls'? Too patronising for words.

He continues, oblivious to my irritation, "Yes that's right, too many people all trying at once. Well I do hope you get in touch with her soon, let me know... Oh yes of course I understand, we can reschedule. Do you want to do it... Oh yes, of course, just let me know. Thanks. Bye. Bye."

"Meeting's off, guys," he says, with no further explanation, "We'll reschedule asap. Now let's try and get some work done if we can. We can keep the TV on if you want. Jerry, I want you to drop what you're doing and find out what you can about what's going on. This is something big, we're going to have to cover it. See if you can get some local angles."

We each go to our desks but I don't think any of us can concentrate. I know I can't. We just keep looking to the TV screen, waiting for more news.

Jerry is busy trying phone numbers, and keeps us updated with what his contacts tell him.

There are rumours flying everywhere, by the sound of it, talk of bombs on trains and bodies on tracks. Apparently the first people had heard, they'd been told there was a power surge on the Underground and that they should use alternative means of transport. As just minutes passed though, there were unconfirmed reports being passed by word of mouth, that there had actually been bombs on the Tube, ranging in number from twelve down to three. Then there was this London bus that was said to have exploded, or was it two London buses? It seems that people are being told to stay put – at home, at work, wherever they are. This must be something big, to bring the city of London to a halt in this way.

I can't believe that the big news of yesterday, of the Olympics coming to London, has been eclipsed in such a way. I think back to the radio presenter going on about it as I drove Dave to the station just this morning. Somehow that seems so long ago.

I sporadically try to call Dave's mobile but still nothing's happening. I am just going to have to wait it out.

As the day wears on, more details unfold on television about the explosions and it's confirmed that these were indeed caused by bombs and that the correct number of them was four – three on the Tube and one on a bus.

From a selfish point of view, it's kind of comforting to know that, according to the news, there are thousands of people out there who have also been unable to contact their loved ones. It's also a huge relief to hear there are apparently no confirmed deaths as yet.

The footage on TV shows a city shocked though, and I'm sure that nobody in Britain can help but be stunned by this, whether they have personal reasons to worry or not. Although it appears to be on a smaller scale, it really does feel like September 11th 2001. I remember how everyone had just seemed unable to stop watching the news then – those people throwing themselves from the windows, the fireballs as the planes ploughed resolutely into those buildings. That's what I remember most. That and those huge towers of trade falling to their knees.

It seems that in these situations people, including news teams, cling to familiar phrases. With September 11th, it had been how getting on an internal flight in the States was like getting on a bus over here (somehow more significant now). With this, it's the symbolism of the London bus. What also strikes me is the use of the word 'cowed' by politicians and others in the public eye. Tony Blair is the first to use it, speaking from the G8 summit at Gleneagles where only yesterday he had been celebrating the success of London in its Olympics bid.

"We will not be cowed."

After he says it, the word seems to be everywhere.

This phrase – the defiance – somehow sticks, maybe because of the slightly unusual choice of words, and I notice it repeated by others throughout the day.

The BBC continues its news coverage; the first survivors' tales begin to come in. People near the explosions, at the stations or near Russell Square, where the bus had been blown up. Footage of people searching crowds for familiar faces, missing friends and relatives. Roads chock full of stationary cars, buses, vans. People walking home for perhaps the first time ever, using maps to find their way on the unfamiliar streets that they are more used to travelling beneath. People's reactions to the events, angered at this attack on their city but amazingly strong and united in their resolution to just keep going. They will still get on the Underground when it's running again. They will carry on as normal.

The people of London look bemused and bewildered but the people of London, it seems, even in their initial disbelief, are resolute that this will not change anything. They will not be cowed.

Chapter Five

What a shocking, sickening day. Nobody can take it in, and nobody can take their eyes off the TV screen. It's wall-to-wall footage of London. The same pictures of emergency services trying to make their way through traffic-clogged streets are played again and again.

I sit at my desk and try to write up some notes but there's no way I can concentrate. Surely Guy is going to have to re-think this week's edition anyway? Although we are a local paper, if something of this magnitude happens on the national or international stage, we usually have to change tack and come up with 'local angles'.

The main problem with this that I can see is that, at the moment, the two immediately obvious people who may have personal stories to tell are me and Guy. That is being terribly pessimistic of course, but despite the blazing sunshine, bright blue sky and twinkling sea which confidently fill the peeling painted frame of the office window, today is not really a day for optimism.

Guy looks at me as he comes out of his office.

"Still not got through to him, eh?"

"No, no, not yet," I answer impatiently, irritated even though I know it is unfair, especially given that Guy is having similar worries to mine.

"Well, look, I'm sure you will. Let me know, yeah? Why don't you head off for now though, eh Jamie? I think we've got everything covered. Isn't that right, Jerry?"

Jerry looks at me and smiles, "Go on Jamie, I'm sure you'll be hearing from Dave soon. Why don't you go and clear your head a bit though? Have a walk on the beach or something? It's got proper stuffy in here this afternoon."

"OK, I will," I give them both a small smile, grateful for their kindness.

Sheila also asks me to let her know when I hear from Dave. I know it sounds daft, and I'm probably worrying unduly, but I am aware that by now all of the mobile networks are back up and running, and yet I still can't get through to him. His train was due into London not that long before those bombs went off. I can't help but worry.

When I call Dave now, it's going straight to his voicemail so it is obviously connecting, and I've left at least five messages. Most times I hang up as soon as I hear "Hi, this is Dave Matthews…"

I take Jerry's advice and walk down to the beach. What a contrast from those scenes on TV. It's July and the holiday season is in full swing. I wonder if these people have even heard what is going on in London? Although the schools have yet to break up for summer, there seem to be a lot of kids around, shrieking and splashing in the sea, building complex sandcastle structures and kicking sand at the gulls. That never fails to annoy me, even though I know the gulls are a pain.

I think perhaps this is not the place for me today. I phone my parents and Mum answers.

"Oh love, come on over, of course. Do you know, I'd forgotten Dave was in London today. He'll be fine, you know. Just keep trying. I'm sure he'll phone you soon anyway. Get yourself up here. You can have your tea with us if you like."

I walk over to Mum and Dad's. It's a steep hill up to their house, on the opposite side of town to my flat. I put my head down and walk quickly, whereas usually I take my time and enjoy the opportunity to look back over the town's houses spilling down the hill and into the bay.

I just want to see Mum and Dad. I'm concentrating so hard on getting there as soon as I can that I almost miss the sound of my phone in my pocket.

I snatch it up quickly, answering it without looking at the display. "Hello?"

My voice is breathless, partly from the hill and partly because my heart is practically in my throat. Before I even hear the voice on the other end I feel relief start to rush through me.

It stops abruptly; "Jamie? It's Mel."

My heart sinks back down to where it's meant to be; maybe even a little lower. The relief retreats through me, like a wave pulled back by the tide.

"Hi." I don't know what else to say.

"Are you OK, Jamie? Is Dave OK? Isn't he in London today?"

"He is, yeah, how did you know?"

"Erm, I think you mentioned it at the weekend. Have you heard from him?"

I don't remember mentioning Dave's trip to Mel but I guess I must have.

"No, I haven't. I'm sure he's OK though," I add, falsely bright.

"Well the phone networks are all down you know."

"They were," I answer dully, "They're back up now."

"Oh. Right. Look, I'm sure he's fine you know. Do you want me to come over and keep you company till you hear from him?"

"No, it's OK, I'm going up to Mum and Dad's."

"Alright, well look, I'll get off the phone, he might be trying to call right now! Give me a ring when you hear from him, OK?"

"Thanks Mel, I will."

I've stopped while I'm talking to Mel, leaning on the stone wall which separates the street from the graveyard. I look over the carved white stones, the graceful angels keeping watch over the graves; the ornate crosses and the smaller slabs, some damaged and many mossy and darkened with age. Beyond, the dazzling white sand meets the cold, confident blue sea which floods towards the horizon. Even now, the sea draws me and I find myself longing to be submersed in it. Letting the waves wash over me, diluting my fears and worries.

Gulls cry to each other as they fly overhead, attracting the attention of a crow which comes charging through the sky from its nest in a tall leafy tree, flying straight at the bigger birds and attacking them until they scatter, squawking but not looking back. The crow returns to its nest.

I try Dave once more but again I get his voicemail. I have no idea what's going on. I keep repeating to myself that the chance of anything having happened to Dave is tiny, but I can't seem to shake this bad feeling that I have. Surely he should have called me by now to let me know he is OK. Before I had left work there had begun to be unconfirmed reports of the odd fatality from the bombs. These reports sent a chilling shiver down my spine, but I somehow can't separate out my worry for Dave and concentrate on the victims of the crash.

Not until I know for sure that he was not one of them. I don't know if this feeling of foreboding is just a natural effect of such horrific events rather than some kind of sixth sense telling me my boyfriend is in trouble.

At Mum and Dad's, our family dog Sam comes slowly across the garden to greet me, hindered by his aged bowed legs but propelled by his wagging tail. A border collie from working parents, we got him from Simon and his dad on Oakdale Farm when I was twelve, so Sam is knocking on for seventeen now. His fur is grey around his muzzle and ears and looks dull and unkempt where once it was glossy. I crouch down to make a fuss of him and he licks my ear.

Mum appears round the corner with a box of soil-covered vegetable she must have just picked.

"There you are, love. Any luck yet?"

"No, not yet."

I keep rubbing Sam, squeezing back the tears which have sprung up at the sight of my mum. There's something about her that always brings my true feelings out but I don't want her to see I'm upset and I don't want to be upset.

I smile at her and straighten up. We walk to the back door with Sam following on, unwilling to be left out.

"I can't tell you for sure that Dave's OK," Mum says, "But I'm sure he will be. You just don't know what's been going on in London today. Anything might have happened. Although I suppose that's the problem."

"I'll keep on trying to call him. I just know that he was due into London not that long before the explosions and I know he'd have been getting the Tube – he'd have had to. I wish I'd paid more attention to what he was doing, where he was going."

"Have you tried the helpline that's been set up? Just to put your mind at rest, I mean?"

"I will do, if I don't hear anything soon."

Dad arrives home from work while I am on the phone to the helpline. Mum has evidently already told him what's going on as he comes in, smiles at me, and quietly kisses me on the head then leaves the room.

The man on the end of the telephone is very kind and very calm. I give him Dave's details and he searches the information they have at present but finds nothing. It's very limited right now, he tells me, but they are working hard to build a picture of today's events and they will contact me if they hear anything. For now the best thing I can do is keep trying to contact Dave myself and try not to worry. He says that if I had plans to go to London to try and find Dave myself, I should forget about them and stay put. The best thing I can do is stay at the end of the phone and of course to let them know when (if) Dave turns up.

Mum, Dad and I eat our dinner sitting in front of the TV. Despite his age, Sam has lost none of his ability to play the old sympathy card and sits in front of me, shuffling up closer in what he believes to be a subtle manner, until he is able to put his head on the cushion next to my leg.

He looks up at me with his soft brown eyes, giving the impression that he hasn't eaten in weeks. Even after sixteen years he's convinced this trick will work some day. I smile as I gently push his head off the seat, and he doesn't complain. With my sleeve pulled over my hand, I rub at the small pool of saliva he has left.

Predictably, all TV stations are focused on London. We watch people out on the streets with photos and posters of the missing. Walls are already plastered with pictures of people. Some of the crowd speak to camera, appealing for help, telling their stories, giving names and descriptions, desperate for information. These people must know for sure, I think, that the people they are looking for were on those trains or that bus. They must have a good idea. Again I wish I had paid attention to Dave's plans but we aren't really like that – I don't need to know all the minute details of his life. I knew he was going to London, I knew he was coming back. That seemed to cover everything.

After tea, I decide to go back to the flat and see whether he's called there. I'm tired and I am fed up of seeing the same footage being played over and again. Dad offers me a lift but I think the walk will do me good.

I return down the hill. The sun is lower than when I was walking up, but there are still hours of daylight left. On the beach I can see a couple walking together, holding hands. It makes me think of the first time Dave came to see me. Only ten months ago. It seems to have passed so fast and at the same time it seems so long ago.

I arrive home to hear my telephone ring off. I dial 1471, hoping of course for Dave's number, but it comes up as withheld. Then my mobile starts to ring in my pocket.

The screen reads 'Withheld Number'. It could still be Dave. Maybe he's calling from a hotel or something.

"Hello?"

My breathing is shallow, as if I have run up a flight of steep stairs.

"Is that Miss Calder?"

"Yes… speaking…"

I feel my blood run cold through me, and tiny bumps prickle all over my skin.

"This is PC Brown from the City of London police. We believe we have some information relating to Mr David Matthews."

Chapter Six

I sit shaking, back against the wall. I am barely able to respond. I listen to PC Brown speak.

She tells me that they have a man in intensive care, and amongst his possessions is Dave's wallet. They'd checked the database and found my contact details, and they need me to come and identify him.

Intensive care, I think to myself, my head feeling light and empty. My vision blurred though I don't think it is from tears. I don't feel real enough to cry. I can't speak.

"Are you alright, Miss Calder?"

"Yes," I manage to whisper, "But are you sure it's Dave?"

"I'm really sorry but we're not able to confirm anything at the moment. This is why we need you to come to London. I'm terribly sorry for the inconvenience."

I wonder why they are unable to confirm whether or not it is Dave. Is it standard procedure or is the person too injured for recognition? Surely otherwise it would be possible to check against the picture on his driver's licence or something?"

"Miss Calder? Are you still there? Will you be able to come to London? Can somebody bring you?"

"I think so; my parents. I'll call my parents."

PC Brown tells me the name and address of the hospital and the ward, and gives me her number to get in touch when we're nearby. She will be on shift all night and will meet me and accompany me when I go in to see Dave. She is kind and concerned, I can tell, and she must be having a traumatic time herself.

"Thank you, I'll call you." I put the phone down, feeling a rush of panic and urgency overwhelm me. I pick up the phone to call Mum and Dad, fingers shaking with fear and adrenaline.

I knew it, I think to myself. I just knew something wasn't right. How long will it take to get to London? Five hours? Six hours? What will

I see when I get there?

Mum answers the phone, and momentarily goes quiet as I blurt it all out. She shouts to Dad and I hear her telling him what's going on. I remain quiet at my end of the call, trying to calm my breathing, as they decide that Dad will come and pick me up, and she can explain to his work tomorrow. She tells me to pack a bag in case we need to stay over.

"Thanks Mum."

"Nothing to thank me for, just take care of your dad for me! Love you, Jamie."

I love my mum's ability to remain calm and cheerfully pragmatic. It is a side not everybody sees because she is relentlessly nice to everyone but she is an incredibly strong and sensible person. I call Guy's work mobile, and leave a message telling him I won't be in the following day, with the vaguest of details. I don't really want everybody talking about this behind my back.

Within 15 minutes, Dad draws up outside the flat. I am already waiting, bag in hand, and I get into the car. He puts his hand on mine and asks if I'm OK – the most futile and yet most natural question to which we both know the answer is no.

As we drive out of town, the stars seem to pop one by one out into the inky sky, mirrored by the twinkling lights of boats still out on the dark sea, waiting for the tide to turn so they can return to harbour.

On the radio, the bombings are all anybody can talk about. Any music they play is slow and sad, like the time when Princess Diana died.

I flick through the channels until Dad hands me his CD case with a sympathetic smile. It's impossible to find something I want to listen to though, and I find myself switching the stereo off altogether.

Tonight the sounds of the car engine and the wheels on the road are more appealing to me, as we travel into the forbidding darkness of the Cornish countryside. In the dark, Cornwall seems different. The county I love, to many just a holiday destination, changes. During the day it is all upbeat sunshine, sand and sea, but at twilight, away from the resorts and the busy tourist pubs, it becomes eerie.

There is a lot of untold history here, and dark secrets. Woodland becomes oppressive in the dark and the gentle hills loom up like silent threats. The moors are empty and lonely, as the wind whistles across them with its whispers of shipwrecks and people lost to the sea.

We don't talk much. Dad makes the odd comment about how long it will take us to get there, and the roads being empty. I don't think a journey has ever seemed so long.

Dad yawns from time-to-time and I think how tired he must be. My own eyes are sore and long to close but my mind will not let them. It runs rings around itself, imagining all possible outcomes. I imagine Dave being dead by the time I get there. I picture his funeral, what I would say. How I would feel. I imagine him brain damaged, or losing a limb, or ending up paralysed. I try to see myself looking after him. Or sitting by his bed all night as machines blink and beep, telling us he is just alive. No matter how hard I try, I can't seem to imagine a happy outcome.

As we cross the border into Devon, we stop at a service station for fuel. Dad buys crisps and chocolate and makes me eat some but they seem to clog up my nervously dry mouth and throat. They make me feel sick. I drink some water while Dad stretches his legs and sips at a scalding coffee.

"Are you alright, Dad?" I ask, looking at his face as he gets back in the car. He looks shattered and, despite my preoccupation with the situation, I feel my love for him pulling at me.

He smiles at me and hands me his coffee.

"I'm fine, Jamie, don't worry. I'm more worried about you; and Dave. I'm sorry this journey's taking so long."

Typical Dad, apologising for something totally out of his hands.

"Thanks, Dad," I whisper, tears springing afresh in my sore eyes.

"I've been thinking though, shouldn't we have got in touch with Dave's mother? Let her know what's going on?"

The thought hits me like a fist. Dave's mum. Strange though it may seem, I have never actually met her – or spoken to her. I now think that seems really weird. I hadn't really thought about it till now; I guess that things have just moved so fast with Dave, I've never really given it much thought. He doesn't talk about his family that much so I have always assumed they are just not very close. His dad is not around, I know that much. Needless to say, I don't have a contact number for Dave's mum. How awful, I think, but what can I do? Maybe it's better that I find out what's happening first anyway, but then I know my own parents would want to know what was going on if the situation was reversed. Perhaps when I meet PC Brown she'll know how to find a contact number.

"Don't worry, Jamie," Dad says, "Maybe the police will have managed to contact her already, you never know. For the meantime, we need to just keep on going."

Once more, we pull out into the blank dark of the night, which is punctuated occasionally by the headlights of cars coming the other way. I know Dad is glancing at me from time-to-time, and I know the concerned expression which is on his face without even looking at him. I can't look at him. I feel, strangely, almost embarrassed by this situation. It has a feeling of melodrama somehow, which I would really rather my life went without. Unlike some people who seem to thrive on creating a drama, I am quite content to have as smooth and straightforward a life as possible.

It's weird, sitting in a car for hours, when you're dying to get somewhere. Not even driving, I feel useless and impotent. I can feel my shoulders and neck muscles starting to ache. I try consciously to relax, to rest my head back, but just moments later I realise I am hunched forward again. Like it means I will be in London quicker.

Mum calls us at about half one in the morning. I suspect she hasn't been to sleep.

"Not far now, Mum," I say, "We're nearly on the M25."

"And are you OK; and your father?"

She is naturally worried for Dad, driving this huge distance after a long day at work and with no sleep.

"I'm fine!" Dad shouts, and smiles at me.

"We're both OK, Mum, thank you. I'll call you as soon as we know anything more. Now go to bed; at least one of us should be getting some sleep."

Finally, we enter London. I can't believe we are here and now I start to feel a sense of reluctance, like I actually don't want this car journey to end after all. This is comfortable and familiar: Dad and I cocooned in the soft safety of the car. I'm well aware that when I get out, when we get to the hospital, my life may very well change forever. I don't think I'm ready for it.

London is strange. There is a very obvious police presence, and sporadic groups or couples, yet the streets seem hushed. I try to match it to the pictures we saw on TV just hours ago. It seems like days ago. Soon this city will be waking up with a terrible, thumping hangover, stunned and disbelieving, struggling to come to terms with the previous day's events.

We arrive at the hospital but can't see anywhere to park. We drive along a couple of streets before we find a metered spot. Not the time to think about car parking charges.

There are more people around the hospital and I realise that many of them must be people like me. We still don't know how many people were injured or died but multiply the figure by two or three for the people who would be visiting them in hospital or identifying bodies. These are the people who are all around us now.

There are police everywhere too. The atmosphere is like nothing I have experienced before. There is talk everywhere and a sense of urgency and fear. Dad and I walk in silence and we stop amidst the smokers outside the main doors to the building so that I can call PC Brown.

Voicemail.

I can't believe the number of times I have got through to voicemail today. I leave a message, then I try again straight away and this time I get through.

I explain who I am; I realise I must be one of many to her. She tells me to wait where I am and she will come and meet us.

After about five minutes my mobile starts ringing and before I answer it, it rings off and I see a policewoman who looks younger than me walking towards us.

"Jamie Calder?"

"Yes, that's me. And this is my Dad."

"Hello, I'm PC Brown. I hope your journey hasn't been too bad. It's a long way, especially at this time of night."

Why is she talking about the journey? Who cares? I want to see Dave.

"Follow me, we can go somewhere for a quick chat. I know how anxious you must be."

We follow her in silence, just two more worried people amongst hundreds. There are police everywhere in the hospital too and medical staff rushing about.

"In here," PC Brown smiles at us and opens a door into a small room with two chairs and a desk. She perches on the desk and Dad and I obediently sit down, looking at her expectantly.

"Now I just wanted to prepare you before we go into the ward," her phone rings, she checks the screen briefly and cuts the call off, "Sorry about that. There are a lot of people in here, in a bad way. The staff are doing their best but they've got so many people to treat. Please try to be calm when we go on the ward."

"What about Dave?" I blurt out, "How is he?"

"The patient is unconscious," PC Brown tells us, and I wonder at her choice of words which seem quite cold to me, and distant, "He was brought out of the tunnel unconscious and has not regained consciousness as yet, which is part of the reason it was so urgent for you to come and see him – to confirm his identity. I do understand you want to see him but please be prepared for the injuries he's sustained, which are quite severe. He is in a stable condition, but you won't be able to stay on the ward very long. I'm sure you understand the staff here are extremely busy, having to cope with an extreme number of casualties. Have you got somewhere you can stay tonight?"

"We'll sort it out," says Dad, "Now can we go and see him?"

"Of course sir, we'll go in now."

I feel like I've been living on my nerves for days. My jaw is clenched tightly and Dad takes my arm as we walk to the lift with PC Brown. We get in and go up two floors. Down a corridor, through two sets of swing doors and we are on the ward. Here are the beeping and blinking machines I imagined. Hushed voices of doctors and nurses discuss patients and treatments. People are hooked up to drips, bandaged, immobile and unconscious.

"It's the bed at the very end," PC Brown tells us, "Please follow me."

Morbidly, the words 'the end' strike a chord with me.

Time slows as I follow the policewoman forwards, deliberately averting my gaze from the other beds, the other patients. Dad is right next to me but I don't dare look at him either. I am trying, desperately, to prepare myself for what I am about to see. Our footsteps sound louder than they should and I can hear my quickening heartbeat resounding in my head. I realise I am holding my breath and I try to let it out slowly, to help calm myself.

I can see the bed at the end now, partially obscured from view by a white-coated doctor checking on one of the other patients. The doctor moves and I have a clear line of sight.

The man on the bed has his face turned slightly away from us, and I can see curly dark hair poking through the bandages around his head.

My stomach sinks.

I know immediately, without a shadow of a doubt.

This isn't Dave.

Chapter Seven

I open the top of the fish tank and watch the ghost of a flake of food swirl around in a slow, lonely waltz on top of the water. I hadn't even wanted fish but Dave had bought them for me. Right now it feels like they are the only link I have with him. Proof that the strong, steady relationship I believed I had was actually something quite different.

I never questioned that I knew so little about my boyfriend's past; stupidly, I didn't think it was relevant. If I could have foreseen what was going to happen I may have made more effort but, let's face it, he was interested in me. I was interested in talking about me. He seemed reluctant to go into any detail about his family, previous girlfriends, even friends, and I didn't push it. Now, with a lack of facts or even clues, I am left playing a futile guessing game which I think may be slowly driving me mad.

The moment we saw 'Dave' in the hospital bed, there was confusion. Dad continued towards the bed while I stopped dead in my tracks.

"It's not him," I managed to hiss. Dad looked around.

"What do you mean?" he asked, "How can you tell? You can hardly see him."

"The hair," I tell him, "This bloke's got hair."

I became breathless, faintly aware of how ridiculous I sounded. The fact was, I had shaved Dave's head for him the previous weekend. This was the first, most immediate thing about the person in the hospital bed which sprung to my mind, and surprised me in doing so as I had not consciously been thinking this at all.

Of course in just a few passing moments, this was not the only thing about the man in the bed that told me it wasn't Dave lying there. Despite a similarity in height, the shape of this person was all wrong. This guy was much slighter than my boyfriend. Looking intently at the unknown person, I tried to feel sorry for him – here was, after all, someone else's boyfriend perhaps, or friend or brother; somebody's son. I couldn't really feel it though; I just felt deflated.

Where was Dave? What had happened to him? I was aware of my vision going fuzzy and flooding with darkness. I realised I was falling towards Dad.

I only passed out for a few seconds. I opened my eyes to see Dad crouching over me. He and PC Brown helped me out of the ward.

"Are you sure it's not him, Miss Calder?" the policewoman asked.

"I'm sure, I should know."

"Of course, of course," she said, placating me. I bet she wished she'd become a teacher instead of a policewoman. How could she have imagined this terrible day though?

"I think the best thing you can do is find a hotel and get some rest," she told us, "Let me know where you are and I will see if I can find out what's going on."

Dad thanked her and we went out into the already-warm early London morning. I was somehow surprised by the daylight; it felt out of place. These events demanded darkness, not cheery sunshine.

We walked to the car and got our bags, trailing listlessly through the streets, past the rows of buildings darkened by city smog and streaked with pigeon shit, until we found a small, shabby hotel which had an extortionately-priced grimy twin room.

It has come out by now that a number of London hotels sympathetically hiked their prices up on the night of July 7th. Which I guess is how we came to pay close to £150 for this place. As it was well after 5am by this point and check-out was at 11am, we barely had a night there anyway, but Dad was shattered from the long drive. While the kettle boiled he rang Mum to let her know what had happened, then rang PC Brown and left her a message telling her where we were. I sat hunched up on the small chair, shivering. Dad made me drink some hot chocolate with extra sugar. I could tell he didn't know what to say; he was as confused as I was, and from the way he kept rubbing his eyes I could also see he was tired out. I told him to get some rest, and agreed I would too.

Pretty much from the minute Dad lay down, he was snoring quietly, and I envied him his ability to sleep, for I don't believe I managed to at all.

At some point, there was a delivery to the hotel. Judging by the sound of it, the hotel had requested that all of the bottles they had ordered be smashed into tiny pieces upon arrival.

The careless racket would normally have annoyed me, especially having forked out £150 to stay somewhere, but on this occasion it was somehow soothing. The sound of life going on, no matter what.

I lay with my eyes scrunched slightly against the bright light of day, in my head growing more and more confused and frantic, trying to work out what was going on. From time to time I tried Dave's mobile again but as always, it just went straight to his voicemail.

Who the hell was that bloke in the hospital and what was he doing with Dave's wallet? There must have been some mistake; perhaps it had been found near him. Or perhaps some incompetent idiot had mixed up everybody's belongings. Maybe this was happening to loads of people, maybe nobody had the right identity. Perhaps Dave actually was lying in that same hospital, confused with somebody else. For all I knew, I could have walked straight past him. The one thing I was sure of now though, was that Dave had been on that train. What that might mean I could only imagine. Again and again and again.

Dad woke at about half past eight. He looked about him, momentarily confused, then looked at me, immediately alert.

"Are you alright, love?"

"I think so."

"What time is it?"

"It's still early, get some more sleep if you like."

"No, I don't think so. I feel better for that little kip," he smiled at me. I tried to smile back.

"What shall we do, Dad? What do we do now?"

I could feel the tears welling up and Dad came over, wrapping his arms around me and wedging himself onto the edge of the tiny bed.

"Shhh, it's OK, it's going to be OK."

I felt like a little girl again, and I let the tears come as I buried my head in my dad's shoulder. My shoulders heaved and I cried loudly and unashamedly while Dad rubbed my back.

A wave of deep fatigue washed over me and I could feel my eyes trying to close but I wouldn't let them. What use was sleep now? I thought of the people I had seen on TV, posting pictures of their loved ones on walls. Searching. Hoping. I wished I'd thought to bring a picture of Dave with me. At least then I could be out there trying to actually do something.

"What do you want to do, Jamie? Do you want to stay in London or go home? I'll do whatever you want."

Dad's kindliness brought my tears flooding back once more. I didn't know. I couldn't see how I could go home till I had found Dave. But how to do that?

"Perhaps you could call PC Brown again?" I asked in a small voice.

"OK, no problem. Stay there." Dad propped me up against the pillows and got his phone from his bedside table. He dialled the number but got no answer. He left her a message asking her to call him back.

"Let's go and get some breakfast," he said.

I had no wish to eat, could not think of it, but it was important for Dad to get something. I drank a cup of strong coffee while Dad had a bowl of cereal and a yoghurt and tried to persuade me to eat something, to no avail. Just the coffee made my stomach churn.

We eventually heard back from PC Brown at about half past ten, just as we were deciding whether to head home or not. She apologised for not being in touch sooner but had been trying to straighten things out, she said.

It transpired that the man who was not Dave had been identified; not so much a man in fact, as a teenage boy. He had come round enough to tell them his name, which they matched with the details his mother had given to the helpline. He had been prosecuted for theft in the past, specifically pick-pocketing, and so it was assumed that this kid had stolen Dave's wallet from him. Where the boy's own belongings were, it wasn't clear. It would be a while before they could question the boy properly, so the details were still unconfirmed, but the explanation did kind of make sense.

Unfortunately it helped not at all in answering the one question I couldn't escape. Where was Dave?

PC Brown was terribly apologetic about the mistake, but it didn't matter. I had somehow gleaned a small seed of hope from what she said – perhaps, if this man had stolen Dave's wallet, he had done it before he got on the train. Dave may be out there somewhere. He could even be heading home to Cornwall right now.

Dad seemed to read my thoughts,

"Don't get your hopes up too much, love," he told me kindly, "But let's go home shall we? It's no good hanging around here."

I agreed, although part of me felt guilty, thinking perhaps I should stay there, walking the streets and searching. I hardly knew London though, and when I looked out of the window at the busy, dirty street below, I couldn't help but picture Cornwall in my mind. The pull of the place, I felt it even then. The peace. The sense of time. I wanted to be back home.

The fish start to dart upwards, checking for new food. I feel dazed and my eyes and body ache with exhaustion. Utterly drained, nothing makes sense.

I take the tub of fish food and empty a tiny shovelful onto the water. The fish begin greedily consuming it, making small 'plip' sounds as they snatch the flakes from the surface.

It's been a week now and yet no word from, or about, Dave. It seems as though the dead (there are around 50 apparently) and injured have all been claimed. So what of my boyfriend? What has happened to him? PC Brown has been in touch a couple of times; she's confirmed that the boy in the hospital bed did indeed steal Dave's wallet from him.

The boy is now in recovery and will be charged with the crime but to be honest I hardly care about that. The thing that does annoy me about it is that Dad and I made that journey to London, all the while thinking that Dave was injured but that at least we knew where he was.

It is not the boy's fault that we don't know Dave's whereabouts though and to be honest I am too tired to care overly much about why he stole Dave's wallet. PC Brown tells me that the police are hanging onto the wallet for now as evidence.

I have explained to her about Dave's Mum and if she is surprised that I don't know this fairly basic detail about my boyfriend, she doesn't show it. I guess she experiences all sorts of situations in her job. I do feel sorry for her; she must be dealing with such a lot of different people at this time. She must be exhausted.

We've checked with hospitals for other fatalities and other injured people – despite the fact that the country seemed to stop on July 7th, there were of course still other everyday incidents occurring - road accidents, street robberies – and it's possible that Dave could have been caught up in something else. The CCTV from the Underground stations is still being worked through so I am hopeful that may possibly hold a clue, but so far nobody seems to have seen Dave.

I have looked through his belongings in my flat, realising for the first time how few he brought with him. Considering he had moved in with me on a permanent basis, and that he has not lived with his mum for over twelve years, where is all the crap that accumulates over this length of time? My flat is full of my useless clutter; things that I can't quite bear to throw away, or can't quite be bothered to clear out. I was sure there must be an address book, something to connect me to his life before he came here, but there is nothing.

I guess he used his laptop and his mobile to store his information, and he took them both to London with him. Whenever I try his phone, which is often, it still goes straight to his voicemail. I don't bother leaving a message. I just put the phone down and sigh.

I have spoken to my friend Helen up in Bristol to see if she can provide a link. It was Helen who introduced me to Dave when I went to stay with her for a weekend. She met him through 'a friend' she tells me, and she's now not sure which one, but she asks around, and comes back with nothing. He had just appeared in their group at a party one night, and sort of stuck around. Apparently everybody had assumed he was with someone else, and he was so friendly and laidback that nobody thought to question his presence.

I am angry with Helen, unjustly, for her shallow lifestyle. How is it possible for people to be so unquestioning? This isn't her fault though, I think, and instead I thank her for trying, and put the phone down.

Mel has been here, bringing me flowers, making me cups of tea and offering to stay over. I don't let her. What's the point? I am miserable and poor company right now. Mum and Dad have tried to get me to stay at theirs but I refuse their offer too. I am better off alone for the time being.

They do come over to see me though, and bring Sam with them. To see him struggling to get up the stairs to my flat makes me cry. He is looking up at me, his tail wagging despite the effort it takes for him to climb the staircase; determined to make it to the top, concentrating on getting up to see me.

Mum and Dad have agreed that he can stay with me over the weekend. His company is exactly right for me. I don't have to talk or answer questions. Just his presence is a comfort. I've been trying to help him up and down the stairs to get into the garden when he needs to. He is, as he ever was, patient and kind, his voice rumbling low in his throat to let me know if I am hurting him.

I can hear him snoring in the lounge as I gaze down at these fish, envious of their simple life. I go in and lie beside Sam on the floor, burying my face in his fur. His warmth is comforting, despite the faintly doggie odour. I used to do this when I was younger, if I'd had a bad day at school or fallen out with my family. He murmurs and wags his tail slightly before getting back on with his dreams. I turn the TV on – Sunday night rubbish – and lie there with my dog, feeling his chest rise and fall with each deep sleeping breath.

Lying on the carpet with my head propped up on one elbow and Sam by my side, I wake much later with pins and needles in my right arm and a thick, heavy taste in my mouth. I switch off the TV and stumble to my room, where I sleep heavily and properly for the first time in days.

London Bombings

This week has been shocking, not just for our own nation, but for the world, as a series of bomb attacks on the London transport system has left 52 dead and hundreds injured.

World leaders have expressed their shock and sadness at the events and Tony Blair, speaking from the G8 Summit at Gleneagles, has spoken with calm resolution that our country will not be broken by this or any other terrorism.

Three Tube trains and one red London bus were targeted, apparently by suicide bombers.

Locally, town resident David Matthews, who was in London on the day of the attacks, has been missing since the event and every attempt is being made to discover his whereabouts and ensure his safety.

The thoughts of those at the *Advertiser* and all employees of Avalon Newsgroup are with the injured and bereaved.

Chapter Eight

"Why don't you take some time off work, Jamie?" Mum asks when she comes to pick up Sam, "Just to get your head around things?"

"I don't want to. I'm better off at work, it beats sitting around here thinking. I'd rather be at work."

I repeat this sentiment, in the hope of convincing myself as much as Mum.

"It's up to you," she tells me, giving me a tight squeeze of a hug. "If it's too much for you, though, don't be afraid to tell them."

"I won't. Thanks, Mum."

She goes in front of Sam and I walk behind him as he makes his awkward way down the steps. I can tell it's hurting him. I wish he was young again, and full of life. He used to bound up and down the stairs just for the fun of it when he was a puppy and had mastered this new skill. When he was really tiny he couldn't even get up the one step from the back garden into Mum and Dad's house. I find myself longing for those days again, when Sam was a puppy and I was really just a child. It seems so easy now, so simple, with parents to take care of you and shield you from problems, but then I also remember the frustrations of growing up and the longing to be an adult so that nobody could tell me what to do.

It will always be this way, I think – children in too much of a hurry to grow up and adults craving just a taste of that childish freedom again.

Mum lifts Sam into her car and comes back to give me another hug. I don't feel like crying now; I don't think I could if I tried. Instead, I kiss Mum on the cheek, wave her off and go back up to the flat, to iron my clothes for tomorrow and have a long hot bath.

My ears seem to always be on alert, listening for the phone, wishing Dave would get in touch. I am still guessing again and again at what could have possibly happened. I have checked with the helpline a number of times, just in case, but they have nothing for me. Hospitals – nothing. PC Brown has checked he is not being held in any police station – I don't seriously expect Dave could have been arrested for anything but who knows? He must be somewhere.

I have registered his details with Missing Persons organisations. Everybody is so kind. Some are, I think, a little intrigued by the story too. It is an unusual situation, certainly, and can't just be coincidental that he went missing at the same time as the bombs. The journalist in me knows that my story is one people will be interested in.

Other people seem to have their answers by now – whether they were the answers they wanted or not – and are having to live their lives coming to terms with the truth of their situation.

When I speak to people about Dave, I feel embarrassed admitting that I know so little about him. He lived with me but I had never met his mum, never spoken to her, don't actually know her name (one thing I do know is that Dave kept his father's surname). Dave had no mail coming to this address, other than the odd marketing letter. It had never occurred to me before that this was strange, in fact I don't think it had even registered with me. All I can tell people is that I know he is from Manchester originally and that I think his mum still lives up there.

The one bit of solid information I do have is his previous address in a shared house in Bristol. I phoned up the house myself and none of the people Dave had shared the place with live there anymore. The girl I spoke to was nice and said she thought she had seen some post for Mr D. Matthews but she didn't know if they still had it. I gave her my number and she called back to say she couldn't find it anywhere but she promised to get back in touch if any more turned up.

And that is it. The extent of the knowledge I have of the man I share my life with. Pathetic, isn't it? It's made me start to doubt everything and part of me feels angry at Dave, like he's done this on purpose, while another part tells me not to be stupid; I should be worrying about him, not angry. And I do worry, all the time. I picture him bleeding to death down a dark alleyway. Or maybe Dave was on the train and has not been found, although I know that is not at all likely. He could have been kidnapped – although I don't know why or by whom.

All I know is that anything could have happened to him and I long to hear that he is OK. Actually I long to have him back here by my side but at the very least I want to know that he is well.

I lie in bed listening to the sound of the sea. I usually love this peace and quiet and make the most of any night when Dave is not in bed at the same time as me, as he always insists on putting the radio on. Now though, the quiet is too much, and I find myself putting on Radio 5 just to try and drown out my thoughts. It also makes me feel closer to Dave somehow.

They are of course talking about Thursday's events. I know I shouldn't listen but I can't help it. Just in case there's something, some tiny clue, which might tell me what has happened to my boyfriend. Don't think I'm heartless, please; of course I care about the people who I know have been killed and injured, their families and their friends, but foremost in my mind is Dave. I'm sure most people would be the same.

We know by now that the attack was carried out by Al Qa'eda. Guy's jumped-to-conclusion was actually right. The story is being pieced together and with it come so many questions – why this hatred? How could these people be so sure in their beliefs that it was OK to kill themselves and take away or ruin the lives of hundreds of others?

It does occur to me that this kind of thing goes on in Iraq pretty much every day. A similar number of people, or more, killed pretty much daily. Car bombs, suicide bombs; they're a fact of life there. While this country is shocked to the core, and rightly so, about what has happened in London, we've become used to the stories of similar massacres in other countries, as a sad but inevitable part of the world news every day. The stories all blur after a while and, awful to say, perhaps they become mundane to us for all their frequency.

When people speak about Londoners carrying on as normal, I feel hugely sorry for them and hugely grateful I do not have to live with this kind of threat, but I also wonder about the Iraqi people who have been living with this for so long already. How do they cope? Have they got used to it? Could anybody ever really get used to living with something like this?

Chapter Nine

Life goes on, as the saying goes. And it's true. What else is there to do but carry on? At work I just get my head down and take whatever stories Guy throws my way, hence my name against the tale of the man who got his head stuck in the doctor's surgery sink. Despite everything, I can't deny myself a very small smile at the thought of this – but usually I would be laughing my head off and emailing Russell to tell him all about it. Right now I just don't feel like that but it does all help to take my mind off the thoughts constantly spinning round inside my head.

Still I try Dave's phone. Still no response.

I go to work, I go home. I eat, I sleep, I shower and dress, as if nothing has happened. I now understand what people mean when they say they're on autopilot. I try to keep going as if nothing is different. I keep myself busy, visiting Mum and Dad, walking on the beach, trying to ignore the gnawing feeling inside me. Trying to concentrate on work.

I can't be bothered to cook, and take to either eating at my parents' or getting takeaways.

One night on my way home from Mum and Dad's I witness a disturbing scene on the high street. A taxi driven by Mr Afsar is surrounded by six teenage boys who are pushing, rocking and kicking the car, shouting 'Al Qa'eda' and 'Taliban bastard'.

I feel myself shaking but it doesn't feel like fear. It is a rage, which rises from within and sees me opening my car door and stepping out. One of the boys looks towards me and for a moment I wonder what I am doing but I can't just sit and watch this.

Luckily for me, I think, a group of men appear at the top of the street and the boys laugh with each other as they disappear off down one of the side streets.

I get back into my car. It takes me a while to collect myself. Mr Afsar drives away immediately but I sit and look at the now empty street. Hand shaking, I call the non-emergency police number to tell them what's happened. They promise to look into it. Something tells me that those boys are at least part of the town gang that's been causing so much trouble, but I would find it hard to positively identify any of them if I saw them again.

I go back to my parents'; I just don't want to go home and be on my own again. I don't know what's happening. How can people be abused like that, solely because of the colour of their skin? I'm incensed by the ignorance and the apparent want to hate. One of the ironies of those bombs in London was that they affected all sorts of people of different races, different nationalities and different religions, including Islam.

While we should be feeling more together than ever in the face of these attacks, it appears some of us want to cling even more to the tribal mentality. That weird thing where people feel stronger and safer if they can choose somebody different to themselves to hate. It draws them together and makes them feel superior, I think. At the very least, it makes them feel safe.

You see it everywhere from the classroom to offices, from football supporters to local gangs protecting their turf.

Colour of skin is an obvious visual mark of differences and Mr Afsar is Asian, therefore he of course *must* be Muslim and following this lack of logic, that would make him personally responsible for the bombs in London. Not forgetting September 11th.

I know, I know, logic doesn't come into it. I also know that this gang will target anybody who seems weak or vulnerable. I don't really imagine they give much of a shit about the bombs in London but they certainly make a good excuse for this behaviour. When you think about it, this is actually a total insult to those who have been affected by the bombs.

I feel better staying in my childhood room. It keeps me grounded, this link to my younger life. There are certain songs, books and places which keep me anchored throughout my life and help me feel better in times when I might cast adrift, such as now.

I lie on my back and look up at the ceiling, at the glow-in-the-dark stars I stuck on it when I was about fourteen. They've been painted over but still they glow – more softly and out-of-focus than before.

I think of all the nights I've done this; all the things I've thought about while lying in this exact spot. My first kiss, my school exams, holidays, Christmases, Grandad dying. Things which happened way before I met Dave; things which seemed so important then and most of which have now faded into my history. I wonder if Dave will just be part of my history too.

I gaze at the stars until they blur, until my eyes close. I dream of Dave, of just being in the flat with him. Cooking breakfast together, reading the paper. Nothing big, dramatic, not even romantic. Just being.

That Sinking Feeling

Town firefighters were this week called out to an unusual incident at the medical practice, where a patient awaiting his appointment had to have his head freed from the sink in the Gents' toilet.

Thirsty

The unfortunate chap (who we won't be naming) told staff he had been thirsty so had tried to put his head under the tap but had become stuck and eventually had to shout through for some help. Despite numerous attempts, the reception staff, doctors and nurses alike all failed to work him free and eventually the fire service had to be called in. The sink had to be removed from the wall and the man, who has asked not to be named, has agreed to pay all expenses incurred during the embarrassing incident.

Jane Evans, the receptionist who was on duty at the time, told the *Advertiser*, "I think his pride was hurt more than anything else. I didn't have the heart to tell him there's a water cooler for patients' use in the waiting room."

Chapter Ten

When I wake up it's still dark, and my dream has felt so real that I am happy for a moment - until reality hits and hurts me as if the knowledge and the wound are brand new. I sleep only periodically after this, feeling hot, regularly turning the pillow to find a cool spot to soothe my aching head.

In the morning, Mum brings me a cup of tea. I take it downstairs though, feeling the need for company. Sam lies at the bottom step, his tail lazily thumping the floor in greeting. I eat breakfast with Mum and Dad but barely hear a word they say.

Guy is remarkably kind to me at work. The following week he takes me aside and asks if I would like to hand the gang story over to someone else, thinking it is causing me unnecessary stress.

"I know you've been having a rough time, Jamie, and I'm worried that this is just going to upset you even more. Perhaps you just want to keep your head down for a bit, maybe concentrate on your history series?"

I am surprised by the strength of my reaction to this – having this story taken off me now creates a small panic within. I suppose I'm relying on it to keep me going. I smile at Guy and assure him I am up to the job.

In fact I have a meeting lined up today with a youth worker from St Austell. Jason is a friend of Russell's, from his football days. Russ has put us in touch with each other.

I've been lucky to have been given every single story relating to the gang; following the rise of its influence on the town as the problems progressed from vandalism to assaults on people. I've interviewed a couple whose beloved garden was ransacked, a woman whose daughter's mobile phone was taken from her on her way back from school, and the man who was mugged after he left the pub.

I've also spoken to a lot of people, both on and off the record, about their feelings regarding the problem. People are definitely becoming more scared. There is caution – if not quite fear – when it comes to walking home unaccompanied, where previously people were pretty blasé. Parents fear for their children's safety. Businesses fear for their livelihood as this kind of phenomenon can do all sorts of damage to a town's tourist trade.

The general opinion on the cure for the problem is predictable: catch the little buggers, hang 'em, flog 'em, stick 'em in the army. Impose a curfew. Blame the parents. It wasn't like this when we were young; we had respect for people.

You know the kind of thing.

I don't blame people for their emotional responses. I hate the gang as much as anyone does, but I don't think that this is the answer. I believe that if we are going to solve the problem, we will have to understand it first.

Guy accepts my word for it and tells me he is not going to give me anything else to work on this week. I'm to tell him if (when) I hear from Dave and if there's anything he can do for me, I'm to let him know. You see, Guy's not all bad. Really.

I am glad Guy lets me stick with this and I'm happy that I am still feeling something for the subject matter, and still have energy when it comes to my job.

The next article I am planning is to try to look at solutions to the problem. I know it's going to come across to some as very 'woolly liberal' and no doubt will spark off a number of complaint letters but at least it will get people's attention.

For my own part, I can't just believe that a whole generation of kids are 'bad' or 'evil'. And of course it's the ones off the estate too (or so rumour has it). So are we saying that kids born into poorer families are naturally bad? That it's just in their genes? How could this possibly, logically, be true?

I am looking forward to meeting Jason this afternoon and hearing the views of somebody who has first-hand experience of 'problem kids'.

The rest of the morning passes quietly. I get stuck into some research on various organisations like NACRO and Kids Company, both of whom work with challenging teenagers. Still, it's a slow morning. My mobile is on my desk, next to my keyboard. I glance at it every few minutes, just on the off-chance that a message has come in and I hadn't noticed. It's turning into an addiction, this checking, and it is irritating me but I can't stop. Needless to say, there is nothing. At least now I've got through the feeling of abject disappointment; it's more of an expectant acceptance that Dave is not going to be getting in touch.

The afternoon lifts my spirits. I drive up to St Austell and as I do so, the sun is breaking through the clouds and the faint drizzle which has been coming on and off all morning dissipates.

I meet Jason at his office. He is older than I'd thought he would be and looks quite intimidating, with a broken nose, rugby player's build and shaven head. He is very friendly though and welcoming, and tells me he's really pleased I'm showing an interest in 'his' kids.

I explain to him what is going on in town, specifically the incident with Mr Afsar. He listens to me concernedly, holding my gaze with striking, grey-green eyes. I find myself feeling self-conscious and having to look away from time to time and jot down random words in my notepad.

"Well I'd like to say I'm surprised," he says, "But I've been in this job for over ten years now. It's just constant disillusionment, it's insecurity, it's having parents who seriously don't give a shit about what their kids are doing. It's all sorts of things that affect these kids, but I totally understand that the way they behave makes it impossible for people to feel sorry for them. Most people anyway."

He smiles at me.

"So what do you think you've learned in your ten years?" I ask him, smiling back and thinking how his face has already softened to me. It is good to talk to somebody with compassion, who can look beyond the immediate.

"Well I suppose everything and nothing. I didn't have the best upbringing myself, my Dad was a complete prick and Mum was just a bit ineffectual. Lucky for me I had an uncle to keep an eye on me, got me into football. Mike kept me on the straight and narrow. Didn't let me get away with any bullshit, basically. The kids I work with here haven't always got somebody like that. Don't get me wrong, they're not all from broken homes. Some of them are just... irritating little bastards... but really, they're all just kids. People shouldn't forget what it's like to be a teenager. Hardest time of your life, I reckon."

I think back to my own teen years, which still seem so fresh in my mind. I was a pain in the arse to Mum and Dad at times, but I was also unsure of myself, insecure in my looks, really unhappy at times even though it would be pretty difficult to explain why. I had a lovely home and family – so how much harder is it for those that don't?

"Do you think they're affected by where they live as well?" I ask, "I mean this is Cornwall; people dream of living here, but it's a poor county at the end of the day, isn't it?"

"Without a doubt," Jason says, those eyes on mine again, "And where do these kids live? On the outskirts of towns. On purpose-built estates. Many of what were the workers' cottages – where these people's families would have lived in years gone by – are second homes now, empty most of the year, or rented out to holiday makers. How does it feel to be pushed so far out of the place you come from, to make room for people with loads more money than you? What a kick in the teeth. No wonder they're pissed off."

Jason is leaning forward as he says this. Not aggressive, but enthusiastic. It is easy to see he has very strong feelings in this area.

I know what he's saying; I see it myself in our town. The estates back up on the hill have grown so much since I was a kid, and like high-rise flats, I feel like they are a way of pushing people back. Isolating them from the nice little world of holiday makers, art galleries and cream teas that most people associate with the place.

"Anyway, Russ told me that you're interested in our farm project," Jason says, relaxing back in his chair, "Do you fancy going to see it?"

"That would be great, thanks Jason."

I drive, and Jason directs. By now the sun has pushed away all the clouds so that the sky is clear and the light is dazzling. From time to time I am aware of being alone in the car with a man I don't really know. Or perhaps just with a man who isn't Dave. Not that there's anything going on but there is something about Jason's size and strength that feels overtly masculine, if that makes sense.

Ivy House Farm is about ten miles away from St Austell and the roads soon narrow into single track lanes, with steep sidings of wild flowers and long grasses which shake and shimmer in the breeze that the car creates as we pass by. I keep a careful eye out for passing places which are few and far between; I hope that we don't run into a tractor coming the other way.

We pull into the farmyard, which is rutted and dusty. A collie dog jumps to its feet and comes towards us. Although barking excitedly, its tail is pushed high into the air and its waggling body betrays its friendliness.

"Some guard dog!" I say.

"It's one of Simon's, I think," says Jason, "They're all daft as brushes."

"You know Simon as well, do you?"

"Yeah, not much of a footballer, I've got to say! We've been doing a bit of work together though, thanks to Russ."

I'm about to ask what Jason and Simon are working on when two teenagers – a boy and a girl – come out of one of the barns and Jason shouts a greeting to them.

"Hey, come and meet Jamie," he says, "She's going to make you famous!"

They look at me without much enthusiasm but they grin at Jason.

"She from the paper?" the boy asks.

"Yes, 'she' is," Jason answers sarcastically, "But 'she' has got a name. And she can even talk for herself."

"Hi, nice to meet you," I say, offering my hand and immediately regretting it and the formality the gesture suggests.

Both of them shake my hand though, and the girl smiles at me shyly. She looks at Jason and I think I can see a crush going on right there. Having said that, I think the boy might also have a bit of a crush on the man as well.

"This is Vanessa," Jason says to me, "And this rudeboy is Anthony."

Anthony grins, "Shut up, Jase."

"What, you're not a rudeboy?" Jason pretends astonishment, "Better prove it then, show us around. Jamie might take some photos but don't worry, she won't be taking any of you. Wouldn't want to break her camera."

Vanessa giggles. We head together to the barn they've just come out of, where there are crates of potatoes and onions.

"Are these yours?" I ask, impressed.

"Well yeah, sort of. Not ours. We grew them though, yeah." Anthony looks at his hands as he speaks. Not as confident as he would like people to think.

"Wow," I say, impressed, "What else are you growing?"

"We've done strawberries," Vanessa says, "But they've gone for the year now, and the asparagus too. We're just learning really."

"You like it though?"

"Yeah, I love it," she says enthusiastically, "I thought I hated vegetables before."

"I used to hate vegetables too," I tell her, "But I'm vegetarian now, so can't really get away from them. I've had to make myself like them."

"You do know this place does, like, bacon and sausages too?" Anthony asks me, suddenly grinning.

"Oh, yeah," I answer, "I know that. That's farms for you, I guess. No getting round it."

"Do you want to see the pigs?"

Vanessa leads the way, although the snuffling and grunting are a giveaway to the pigs' whereabouts. We turn the corner to see a small field where about 30 pigs are rooting about, big ears flapping. Vanessa hops over the fence and goes up to one of them, rubbing it behind its front leg. It seems to go into a kind of daze then flops over onto its side. Vanessa jumps back, obviously well-practised at this. The pig murmurs in enjoyment and holds its leg in the air so Vanessa can keep rubbing it.

"You should have seen her when she first came here," Jason leans towards me and speaks so the girl can't hear. I catch a whiff of his aftershave. "She was terrified of all the animals, and we had to pretty much wrestle her out of her heels and bling!"

I smile at this and, watching Vanessa now in her wellies and anorak, her young face free of make up, I marvel at the change which she must have been through.

I also can't help but think again about the way people can form attachments and relationships with animals, yet happily see them killed for meat. I don't get it. I don't think I ever will.

I am not here for my own musings though, I'm here for my work, and what I can see is two very happy teenagers getting stuck into something they most likely would never have had the chance to do without Jason, and without Ivy House Farm.

I climb the fence myself and pet a few of the pigs, then we go to the farmhouse where I interview Vanessa and Anthony, then the farmer, Jack, who turns out to be a friend of Simon's dad.

The border collie, Meg, fusses around all of us during the interview until Jack shouts at her and she shuffles off to sit underneath the table, feeling sorry for herself.

Jack says that he's got nothing but good things to say for the project and the kids who have come to him over the last five years, who he says he now couldn't do without. Aside from one 'bad apple' he says, but he doesn't want that mentioning in the paper because he doesn't want any bad reflections on what Jason and 'the kids' are doing.

When Jason and I leave, we take Vanessa and Anthony back to St Austell with us. Vanessa in particular seems sorry to leave, making us wait while she fusses Meg a bit more. We talk on the way back and Vanessa says she wants to work on a farm. Anthony says he likes it but he wants to work in the music industry really.

After we've dropped them in town, Jason tells me he can't say much about their specific backgrounds but that most of the kids he works with have not had a brilliant time of it – abusive or just plain uncaring parents are often in the picture, meaning these young lives begin with a lack of attention and stability. Predictably this can lead to drug or drink problems, trouble with police, truancy from school. A bad beginning born out of a lack of opportunity, encouragement and, of course, money.

Of course they have to take some responsibility, he says, and that's what his work is about – enabling them to do so and giving them a choice in what they do.

I am quite moved by what he says and when I drop him off I tell him how much I like what he does.

He smiles at me as he leans into the car, those hypnotic eyes catching me off-guard once more.

"I'm glad, Jamie, I hope you'll give us a fair go in your article, then."

I promise I will and that I'll send a copy to him as well.

"Say hi to Russ for me... and Simon," he says, "In fact tell him to pull his finger out and get some of those kids working for him – solve more than one problem, that will."

I realise as I am driving back home that I haven't checked my mobile. I've been too busy thinking about Jason, Vanessa and Anthony. Farmer Jack. What they are doing is brilliant, I think, and yet it's quite simple. The difficult bit, I suppose, is getting people to want to give kids a chance. Especially the type of kids who cause trouble on the streets of their own quiet town.

I'm thinking of Cornwall too, of the sheer beauty of this county. I love the place names in Cornwall - Luxulyan, Lamorick, Zelah, Zennor, Treninnick. Beautiful, exotic names.

It's such a magical place, with its history, clear seas and glowing beaches, but how much does that really mean to those who can barely afford to live here anymore? Those who have effectively been pushed back from their family history, forced inland and back up the hill from the picturesque fishing villages, to make space for the second home owners who come here at their convenience.

Tourists coming and going, splashing out money on holidays and meals in expensive restaurants.

I don't blame the holiday-makers one bit for wanting to come here, and of course they are vital to the local economy, but don't they see that, with the second homes they leave sitting empty for huge chunks of the year, they are effectively driving out the people who want to have just a first home here? Who can't even imagine being in a position to afford two homes. No wonder there is bitterness and resentment.

The problems facing the kind of kids Jason works with, probably the kind of kids who have formed our town gang, are not peculiar to Cornwall by any means. Wherever there is money there is also poverty and where there is poverty I think trouble will follow. Why shouldn't people be angry? Because the anger isn't focused on anything positive, it just breeds more trouble and creates even more of a divide.

It seems so obvious to me. I also feel faintly hypocritical as these thoughts pass through my mind though, for what am I doing, really, to change things? Writing a few articles in a local paper, that's what. How much difference is that going to make in the grand scheme of things?

I consider the landscape as I drive. I pass fields of cows lazily chewing the cud, gathered in groups underneath trees, shading themselves from the heat of the day. Tails swishing away flies.

Swallows line up on telegraph wires before swooping off together. The verges are lined with gorse bushes and tall pink foxgloves, set against a backdrop of gentle dark green hills.

All of this beauty, yet the county hosts dark problems too.

I realise with a shock that my phone is ringing but as I'm driving I can't answer it. All of a sudden my head is full of Dave again, and

I am hoping it is him, though I'm pretending even to myself that I am not really thinking this way. That I know it won't be him. As if by thinking it won't be him, the reverse psychology means that it will be.

I see a lay-by ahead and I pull into it, sending a small flock of starlings scattering into the air. I flick the phone open.

'Missed Call', the screen reads.

My heart is beating fast. I scroll down the screen.

'Sheila'.

My heart sinks.

She's left a message. I'd better listen to it. I try to fight the resentment I am feeling towards Sheila catching me out this way. She would be mortified if she knew, I'm sure.

"Jamie? Can you call me back as soon as possible please?" she sounds a little breathless, "It's your neighbour; Mrs Butters. She's been mugged in town, she's in hospital. They think it's that fucking gang of kids again."

Chapter Eleven

She looks smaller and more crooked than ever, tucked into the pristine white hospital bed. She has a large bruise on her right cheek, merging into a black eye. I feel sick.

The covers are almost uncreased, as though she has not moved at all since being tucked into place. I try not to think of the last, very recent, time I was in a hospital. Keep away, memories, you're of no use to me.

"Hello Mrs Butters," I say, placing the bunch of flowers I have for her on the bedside table, "How are you feeling?"

I try not to look too closely at her face with its rice paper skin, thin frail veins just visible underneath.

"Hello my love," she smiles at me, "Thank you for the lovely flowers, you shouldn't have gone to all that trouble."

"It's no trouble," I say, wondering how it is that people like her always seem to think of others, even in this type of situation. Older people, who think they're a nuisance. As if they don't deserve just as much attention and care as the rest of us.

"What happened?" I ask, and reassure her I've not come in a professional capacity.

"Oh that's good," she says, "I don't want any more fuss."

"Well I can't say there won't be something about it in the paper but we can make sure that the details are kept to a minimum. But I've come to see *you* anyway, not get a story. Do you want to talk about it?"

"I don't know, it just... it all happened so quickly, I don't really know what happened. I was trying to walk back from town yesterday afternoon, with my shopping. It was a dismal day and I was a bit tired, to be honest. So I'd stopped to catch my breath a bit, you know, and then I think somebody hit me. They kicked my shopping over, and took my handbag. Ripped my coat too. I think I, I banged my cheek on a wall. Got a proper shiner, haven't I?"

I feel my heart quicken in anger, and I swallow hard.

"I'm so sorry," I tell her, "I knew the problem had got worse recently but I didn't think they'd pick on..."

"An old lady like me?" Mrs Butters smiles again, "It's alright, you can say it. I am old. I'm nearly eighty, you know."

"So they must feel really big and clever mustn't they?"

"Oh they're kids," she tells me.

"Kids?" I splutter, "No kids do things like this. Kids play in the park, or watch Blue Peter. They don't do... don't do things like this."

"I know," Mrs Butters soothes me, which I think is the wrong way round, "But these are still kids. They don't really know what they're doing. They don't think anyway."

I'm silent for a moment, thinking about what Mrs Butters has said. I can't believe she's being so forgiving, so understanding. It's almost infuriating. Of course they know what they're doing. They are more than old enough to know right from wrong.

"The police came in earlier," She tells me, "Lovely young man by the way, and he told me one of the boys has confessed. His mum took him into the station would you believe! He's reported the other one too, the one who actually attacked me. He was quite upset, apparently. So, you see, they're not all bad are they?"

I sit with her for an hour or so and we watch Countdown together, until Caroline, her daughter, arrives. She's been away with work and has had to rush back to Cornwall although of course Mrs Butters says she needn't have bothered, not on her account.

I discreetly disappear to get some water for the flowers, as Caroline exclaims at the sight of her battered and bruised mother.

Before I go, Mrs Butters asks me to feed her cat, Charlie.

"There's a key under the pot by the front door," she tells me, and as I leave the ward I hear Caroline chastising her mother.

"How many times have I told you not to leave that key there? Anyone can find it."

"And I've told you," says her mother, "I am too old to change. Time was we never locked our doors at all. I've given in to that but if I can't trust people then what's the point in carrying on?"

On the way back to the office I think about the article I'm about to write, about my sympathies with those young deprived people who need a second chance. Do I still believe it? I think so, I hope so. I think of Anthony this afternoon, so committed to his music and his future. I remember Vanessa's shy smile. She's just a girl like I was, but with less of a lucky start in life. She shouldn't be tarred with the same brush as the little bastards who have done this to Mrs Butters.

I make myself remember what Jason was saying about backgrounds shaping behaviour, and also the trouble I got myself into as a teenager. Would I have let myself get so carried away with hunt sabbing that I would have harmed individuals? I don't believe so but I certainly knew others who would; perhaps even did. I was fortunate to get caught out when I did, I think, before I got sucked into that world any further.

I need to keep my word to Mrs Butters about not letting the *Advertiser* make too much of this but it's down to Guy really. Maybe he'll have a bit of pressure to play down this story, though – after all, it doesn't look good for the town, and the last thing we need is to scare tourists away.

This incident would surely make people stop and think, about this idyllic little fishing town, which tourists flock to every year and are ever reluctant to return home from.

As it happens, I don't need to worry too much about letting people know what's happened. When I arrive back at work, Sheila tells me that word has spread already, and that this is the last straw for the town's menfolk.

There is still an old-fashioned, patriarchal side to this place, where there are still 'men's jobs', for example fishing, however in this case I think it has its benefits. Apparently a new gang has formed in the town, this time consisting largely of our volunteer lifeboat crew and a few of their mates. I don't think many teenage boys would fancy their chances against this lot, and word has it that it was actually these local heroes who forced the mate to grass up the boy who attacked Mrs Butters. It's not altogether clear how this happened – whether through physical or mental duress – but it seems to have done the job.

Rumour has it that a full-on search was carried out to get to the bottom of which boys have been involved in the gang from the very start. From there it was a case of catching each one off-guard, when they were on their own so there was no need for bravado, and scaring the bejeezus out of them. It was just a short time before the men had worked out who had been involved in the attack on Mrs Butters. The confession to the police followed soon after.

This is one story which won't be going in the paper, but nobody is likely to make so much of a peep about it. I know it sounds a bit old fashioned but it's not like a lynch mob or something. Just the community facing up to and solving its own problem as it had got to a truly awful point. It's a shame this didn't happen before Mrs Butters was attacked but I feel a slight sense of relief that finally it's been dealt with. Time will tell if it's a lasting solution. There are some big blokes around town though, who I reckon are more than enough to scare some disillusioned and cocky teenagers.

While Sheila and Jerry relay all of this to me, I think again of Ivy House Farm; of Jason, Vanessa and Anthony. I can't help thinking that my article about improving opportunities for the likes of these kids is not going to prove very popular.

Rehabilitation for Troubled Youths

This week I was privileged to spend some time with a youth worker and two of his charges, who spoke openly to me about their backgrounds and about how a local project on a farm near St Austell has helped them to turn their lives around.

One of the teenagers had spent four months in a Young Offenders Institution for stealing a car, at the very young age of thirteen. His background was clearly not the most stable and he had been through a number of care and foster homes, leaving him unsettled and unclear as to his place in society. As the story often goes, he had 'fallen in with a bad crowd' and as a result become involved in crime. He told me that while people had tried to help him, his estrangement from his family had affected him severely and he had not really cared about the people he was harming in stealing their property. He saw being arrested as no deterrent because he was not happy in life. He didn't care if he ended up in jail.

The second teenager, a girl, had been neglected by her family and had been in trouble with the police for shoplifting. She had been drinking heavily since she was twelve, falling in with a gang of older teenagers whom she wanted to impress.

Luckily for both of these two young people, they were referred to the youth worker I met, who has started a project in conjunction with a local farm. On a voluntary basis, the two teenagers work at the farm between two and three days a week, learning skills such as growing vegetables and caring for animals. Both are so positive about their experiences at the farm, and the youth worker who introduced them to it. This affirmative action seems to have made a massive difference in the teenagers' lives and outlooks.

I visited the farm myself and met the farmer, who I can assure you is no pushover, and expects a good day's work from any volunteers, who he provides meals for during their time with him. Having lived all of his life on the farm, the type of background these teenagers come from is alien to him but he told me he is aware of the opportunities he has had in life and he is happy to help provide the same type of opportunities to children who want to do something with them.

This is just one example of an alternative, and positive, way of addressing some of the problems faced within our society. You may wonder why criminal behaviour is 'rewarded' in such a way, rather than being punished. However, even if you cannot sympathise with the poor start in life some children have, and the effect that this has on their behaviour, the undeniable end result of projects such as this is that further bad behaviour is prevented. This can only benefit us all.

** Any views expressed in this article are those of the author and do not necessarily represent those of the *Advertiser* or Avalon Newsgroup **

Chapter Twelve

July turns to August, although not before an apparent attempt at more bombs on the Tube, and the shooting of the young Brazilian Jean Charles de Menezes at Stockwell Underground station.

This is a strange, unhappy time for the country, not only specifically in my life. I feel my grief joining with others'; although perhaps small and insignificant against what they have been through, our sadness merges and swirls together in a thin, almost tangible, mist which lays itself softly across the nation.

There is still no word of, or from, Dave. I have kept on checking with the police, hospitals, Missing Persons, anyone I can think of who might be able to help, but nobody has any information. I think sometimes I'm going mad. To the point of even having imagined what we had, or imaged his existence.

His clothes are still there in the wardrobe though, his toothbrush and razor on the shelf above the sink, along with a few blades of his stubble, which I just can't bring myself to clean away. It would seem symbolic somehow, and I'm not willing to wipe away this trace of him.

Work is keeping me busy. As predicted, my article about the youth project has prompted some responses on the letters page. Nobody has yet written in to comment on the fact that the gang seems to have disbanded. I wonder if they haven't noticed or if we're all supposed to just be keeping a bit hush-hush about the whole thing.

Whatever those men did to the boys, it seems to have worked as there have been no more attacks that I know of. Of course there are still kids drinking and smoking at various locations around the town – bus shelters, benches, down the little alleyways which lead down to the rocks - but no more trouble than that.

Perhaps it was Matthew Browning's arrest that's scared them.

He's been charged and his case is awaiting trial.

His mate, who made the confession, is also awaiting trial, although it is widely believed that the fact that he confessed, and also was apparently not involved in the actual attack (he stood by and watched then apparently was so upset that he was on the verge of telling his mum when the lifeboat crew turned up at his door) means he will not get a custodial sentence.

Mrs Butters is back home with Charlie, and getting on for all the world as if nothing has happened.

I try to match Mrs Butters' strength and also continue with life as normal. Then, one Saturday morning towards the end of August, I get some post from Bristol – a large, brown envelope. I'm not expecting anything and I don't recognise the writing.

I tear the envelope open and inside is a scrawled note from Emma, the girl I had spoken to in Dave's old house, and an envelope addressed to Mr D. A. Matthews.

I hurriedly rip this second envelope open. It is a closing statement for a building society account in the name of one David Adrian Matthews. It shows £8,637 was the closing balance.

I am stunned. Dave and I didn't have a joint account or anything like that, however I had thought we were pretty open about our financial statuses. Evidently not.

The statement shows that Dave's account has been used since he went missing. A lot. In fact, a withdrawal was made in a London branch on the afternoon of 7th July. Reading that date there chills me.

Two further transactions were made in Manchester, then it looks like a return to London, showing a couple more withdrawals of £300 each. Since then it looks like he has not used the account, until he decided for whatever reason that he was going to close it. The trail ends here.

I take a deep breath then tap in the telephone number printed on the top of the statement – surely now I can find out what's been going on. The woman I speak to sounds suspicious of me, and will not tell me anything. Even when I explain to her the situation.

I confirm Dave's date of birth to her to show I'm not making it up. At least I know that much about him.

"Do you have the password?" she asks.

"Is it his mother's maiden name?"

"I can't tell you that."

I didn't know it anyway.

"I'm afraid, Madam, that I can't tell you anything."

She hangs up. I phone Mel.

"Have you told the police?" she asks immediately.

I think of PC Brown and how kind she was. I hope she will still remember me. I dig out her number and my teeth are chattering as I dial it. I feel for the first time that I may actually be getting somewhere with regards to what has happened to Dave.

I blurt out to the policewoman what has happened, and suggest it could be him making the withdrawals – or, after what happened to his wallet, I'm wondering if it could be somebody else. PC Brown talks calmly to me and promises that this will be investigated and she will phone back as soon as she has any news. It may take a couple of days though.

A couple of days? I don't think I can wait that long. I know I don't have any choice though.

I call Mel back and she comes over to see me, insisting that I take a good long walk along the headland with her.

"They've got your mobile number, Jamie," she says firmly, "Sitting around the flat isn't going to make the call come any sooner, you know. And if you don't hear today we'll knacker you out on this walk so that you can at least get some sleep tonight."

Mel is very good and lets me bend her ear on our walk, sounding out various different scenarios. None of them make any sense if they involve Dave though – because if he's OK, why hasn't he come home? Why hasn't he got in touch? I sometimes wonder if he has somehow developed amnesia. Stupid though it sounds, it's the only thing that makes any kind of sense to me, assuming that Dave is alive and well.

"Weird that he had that account and you knew nothing about it," Mel muses.

I fight my immediate, defensive, reaction to this – what is she implying?

"I guess so," I say, "Or maybe he has mentioned it to me before. Come to think of it, maybe it does ring a bell actually."

I can tell Mel isn't convinced and I don't blame her. I wouldn't be, either. Something isn't adding up here, is it? I don't want to think about that now, though.

PC Brown calls later in the day, and I answer nervously.

"Have you found anything out?"

I'm so on edge, I don't even say hello.

"I have, Jamie," her voice is quiet, "But I can't really tell you anything."

"What do you mean?" I ask, incredulous, "Why not?"

"All I can tell you is that Mr Matthews is alive and well."

My heart pounds away. Dave is alive!

"And?"

"And that's all I can tell you. He doesn't want you to contact him."

"What... what do you mean?"

"I'm sorry, Jamie," PC Brown says.

I plead with her to tell me what's happened, or at least to tell me where he is, but she says she can't pass on any more information as Dave has expressly asked her not to. I can tell she's genuinely sorry for me; I can hear it in her voice, but that's of no use to me. I hang up. I run to the bathroom and I throw up.

Mel comes to the doorway and looks at me with such concern I have to look away.

It feels like all of the emotion I've been trying to hold back for the last few weeks is coming out now. Tears are streaming down my face and I throw up, then keep retching until I have nothing left inside me. Mel crouches next to me, holding back my hair, rubbing my back. I sob huge, desperate sobs and hug my knees to my chest, on the cold bathroom floor.

I can't cope with Mel's kindness and I send her home, promising I will call her later. Once I hear her car go, I just sit on the stairs to my flat and I sob loud and hard once more.

After a minute or two, I hear a knocking at my door. I ignore it.

"Jamie? Jamie, dear? Are you alright?"

It's Mrs Butters. I want to ignore her but I can't. I wipe my face on my sleeve and go downstairs. I can see her injuries are healing well, she just has a large yellow ghost of the bruise on her face.

"What on earth's happened?" she asks.

I try to tell her but I start crying again. I'm almost hyperventilating but I don't feel I can do anything to control it. Mrs Butters guides me into her flat, ushers Charlie the cat out of the way, and sits me down.

Gradually I explain to her and she looks at me sadly.

"A little drop of this won't do you any harm," she tells me, pouring a generous glass of whisky. I sip it slowly and she nods in approval.

Charlie jumps onto my lap and pushes his head against my chin. Absentmindedly, I stroke him as I gradually let my new knowledge, or rather lack of such, sink in.

Mrs Butters sits opposite me and lights a long, elegant brown cigarette.

"You don't mind, do you?"

I shake my head.

"Just sit there, as long as you like. You've had a shock."

Sitting here now, I find I don't want to leave her flat. It feels like a different world, but maybe that's just the effect of the whisky.

Her room is hypnotic somehow, though. The ticking clock. The swirls of smoke from her cigarette slowly twirling around the room before being sucked through the open window into the waiting world. The purring of the cat as it contentedly settles itself on my lap.

Mrs Butters doesn't speak, and neither do I. It's nice to feel I don't have to.

In time, Mrs Butters gets up and I hear her pottering about in the kitchen. I feel drained but I feel calm. Eventually, I gently move the cat to the seat next to me and it mutters its disapproval at being disturbed. I have to speak to Mum and Dad though. They need to know what's going on.

I go through to thank Mrs Butters for looking after me.

"It's no trouble, Jamie. It makes a nice change that I can look after you rather than the other way round. You come back any time you like."

She hugs me; she's never hugged me before, and I can feel her elderly body, thin and cool beneath her cardigan. I leave her flat and go back upstairs, with a heavy tread. I phone Mum and Dad. I explain but I have to go through it a couple of times with both of them before they can understand what I'm telling them. The problem is that it doesn't make any sense so can't really be understood. I tell them I don't want company right now.

Instead, I go through the cupboards and drawers and I find everything that belongs to Dave, everything he has ever given me. I pile it up in the lounge.

I get some black bin bags and I go through every item – I read scribbled notes which I, stupid sentimental fool that I am, had stored in my bedside table. Even just silly things like 'Gone to the shops, back soon xxx'.

There are cinema and gig tickets, a receipt from the restaurant we went to on our first date. I can't believe I kept all this stuff. Don't worry, you don't have to tell me I'm an idiot.

Together, all of this stuff creates a potted history of my relationship with Dave. We started with a couple of really romantic, exciting dates in Bristol, which I remember looking forward to so nervously; getting ready for them in Helen's flat, butterflies fluttering in my stomach and doubts playing on my mind. Would he turn up? Did he really like me?

At the end of the night, I'd go back to Helen's and we'd sit up in her bed, chatting. She had just met a new boyfriend too – Mike – and we'd spend hours dissecting our evenings, and congratulating each other on our new-found happiness. I knew Helen and was not surprised when, a couple of months later, she had met somebody new. I was convinced, however, that my relationship was bound to last.

Within a month of meeting, Dave and I were arranging a visit to Cornwall for him, then another a couple of weeks later. I went back up to Bristol but stayed at his house that time, not Helen's. He surprised me by coming to see me again the following week.

Less than three weeks later, he was living in my flat.

I take the clothes and put them in one bag. I can't bear to get too close in case they still smell of him. I don't want that. The clothes can go to a charity shop. CDs and books too. Somewhere well away from here, where I won't have to see them again.

Doing this, I am reminded again of what a shallow presence materially Dave had in my life. There is little else he brought with him. He'd taken his beloved laptop to London of course, and his portfolio. Well I've got a couple of ideas for what he can do with them.

I put the bags by the front door then go back upstairs. I'm crying again now. I'm not sure I have ever been so angry, so hurt, so confused, in my entire life. There is nothing I can do to make this better, nobody to explain it to me.

Going through Dave's things, I am exerting the only, tiny, bit of control I have over any of this. It also feels ever so slightly like I am punishing him, although I am well aware that he isn't here, he doesn't know. He wouldn't care.

In the bedroom, I fall forwards onto the bed, sobbing into the duvet until it's damp beneath my cheek and I feel sick. I lie there in silence for I don't know how long.

No matter how much I go through it all in my head, I can't work out if this is the worst outcome possible. I try to tell myself it would have been worse if he had been killed or injured but somehow I just can't convince myself that's true.

Chapter Thirteen

On I go, on into the Autumn, as the leaves turn yellow, red and brown on the trees and the afternoons rush more quickly towards nightfall, the sun turning its attention to other parts of the world and leaving us to deal on our own with the onset of chilly, misty mornings.

The influx of tourists settles down to a more manageable level. After the intervention of the heroic local men, the town gang seems to have disbanded. A date has been set for the trial of the boys who were arrested for mugging Mrs Butters.

Mrs Butters herself has not let her 'little incident', as she calls it, stop her from going out. She refuses to be cowed.

The shock of the bombs on 7th July has dissipated over the weeks, for most of the country anyway, and life has returned to normal. I still wonder about what it's like living in London now – is it really possible to go back to normal, to not be aware of the threat of a re-run, and put out of your mind what's happened in those tunnels as you travel through on the Tube?

I find people's resilience comforting and inspiring and in the face of what has happened with Dave I try very hard to take the same attitude. Inside though, of course, I am torn through. I just can't come to terms with the apparent cruelty of what has happened and I still can't stop the thoughts going round and round my mind, trying to piece everything together and make some sense of it all.

The feeling of embarrassment persists and I can't bear to talk about it except to Mel occasionally. I just want to put it behind me.

At work, talk has turned to our Christmas/New Year party.

In early January, it is customary for the *Advertiser* to host a drinks party at the White Hart pub for our patrons, clients and local dignitaries. It's a great excuse to charm existing and prospective clients who buy valuable advertising space on the paper's pages; our main source of income. It's also an effective way of getting at least eight pages of the next week's paper filled out with photos of the affair. Easy copy.

It makes me think back to our last party – hard to believe it was just months ago – when I had been so proud to have Dave with me; for the first time, I had a partner to bring to an office party.

Having said that, I may have been better if he hadn't come as he to some extent contributed to a disastrous night. He and Madeleine the student, that is. It was just lucky that Sheila was there, and Simon, Russ's friend from Oakdale Farm.

The night started out OK; Guy showing off, making his inimitable efforts to charm the ladies and the more influential of the local business people. Wherever you were in the room you couldn't escape his snorting and, if he caught me passing by, he would pull me over to introduce me to whoever his lucky companion was, showing off his great relationships with his staff.

"Here she is," he said, putting his hand on my arm and pulling me over to meet the new mayor, Neil Hughes, who is actually a friend of my parents', "Our own Lois Lane."

Original, I think you'll agree.

"Jamie's our brightest star, you know," Guy continued blithely, "Got her fella with her this year haven't you Jamie? We were starting to think she'd be on the shelf forever!"

Neil raises his eyebrows, and gives me a sympathetic smile.

"Thanks Guy," I said, extricating myself from his grip, "Neil's actually met Dave a couple of times already. Nice to see you, Neil."

Guy was taken aback at my familiarity with this town statesman and I took the chance to excuse myself and head back over to Dave, who was sitting with Sheila, her husband Dan, and Madeleine.

Dave seemed to be having a good time, which was a relief, as I know going to your own work party can be hard work, never mind somebody else's. He also seemed to be racking up the drinks, but I didn't think much of it. I'm also prone to drinking a bit too much as a way to make myself at ease on occasion.

I saw Simon across the room, and could see Guy heading his way. I managed to get to Simon before Guy did, and swiftly turned him round, bringing him over to our table. Dan offered to get the drinks in and I made the introductions, noticing Madeleine's eyes seem to light up. Simon is quite a good looking bloke – not particularly your typical farmer, but well built and healthy looking. I wondered if Pony Club Madeleine was looking for a bit of rough.

"Are you OK?" I asked Dave, "Sorry it's a bit of a drag but I have to get on with schmoozing at the moment."

"I'm fine, don't worry," he smiled and squeezed my arm.

I grabbed Sheila, and together we mingled with the guests, making sure Tony, the *Advertiser*'s then photographer, got some good photos of us to go in the paper. To keep things slightly more interesting, all of the *Advertiser* staff excluding Guy compete with each other at these occasions to get in the most published photos. Preferably with a different drink in each one.

At some point, I noticed that the table where Dave had been sitting was empty, and there was no sign of him, Madeleine, Simon or Dan. After an hour or so I began to wonder what had happened to them but Sheila said they'd probably just escaped into the public bar for a bit. I put it out of my mind and concentrated on the photo opportunities.

A short while later, I noticed Dave and Madeleine were back in their seats, looking extremely giggly. I went over to see them and, smelling smoke on Dave, realised they'd been smoking a joint.

I wasn't too impressed to be honest, especially seeing as this was my work party.

"Have you been smoking?" I asked as lightheartedly as I could.

"Ooohhh... don't think Jamie's too pleased," spluttered Madeleine and I felt my irritation rise.

"Yeah, just a little one," Dave said, "Oh come on Jamie, it's a bit dull this, isn't it?"

"I know it is," I said and, looking at Madeleine, "I don't mind at all actually. Don't you think you ought to be doing a bit of schmoozing too though? It's all part of the job you know!"

"Yeah well, I can't be arsed, to be honest. I won't be sticking around this place after graduation anyway. Guy's such a prick, I don't know how you put up with him."

I actually felt quite protective of Guy then, though I realised it was more to do with Madeleine being a pain in the arse and, if I'm honest, the fact she was having a good night with my boyfriend while I was having to behave myself and make conversation with the paper's clients.

I didn't say anything though, and was pleased when Simon and Dan appeared at my side with a tray of drinks, sitting down at the table.

I sat down too, taking the chair next to Dave and cursing myself inwardly for feeling a bit jealous. Madeleine was a lot younger than any of us, and a pretty girl, but when Simon sat down she turned her attentions to him and I relaxed again. Just a small part of me was still ill at ease as I realised Dave was more drunk than I'd ever seen him.

He was being quite rude actually, towards Simon and Dan, and I didn't know if they were picking up on it or if I was being over-sensitive to the situation. It seemed that he was taking the piss out of them, scoffing at things they said, or else trying to outdo any of their stories.

You know when you tell somebody about something you've done and they have to say they've done it too but so much better than you have, or in much more extreme circumstances... or they've had the same illness you've got, but much worse? Well that was Dave that night, and it was a side of him I hadn't seen before.

When he said he was going for a smoke and did anybody want to join him, Madeleine jumped at the chance and the others refused. I felt an urge to join them but checked myself; for one thing I trusted Dave and for another I was at a work function, and needed to remain professional. Nevertheless, as the two of them disappeared outside, I felt uneasy. I made myself get up and go to talk to a new restaurant owner, turning my back to the door so that I wouldn't be keeping half an eye on them returning.

When I looked back to our table, Dave and Madeleine had returned and I felt silly for worrying. I smiled at Dave and he raised his glass to me. Then Guy began ringing a little bell to get everybody's attention as he prepared to make his annual speech.

'Blah, blah, blah, I'm great, the paper's great, but that's only because I run it and I'm great'; that was pretty much the gist of it. He then added a thank you to his clients and his staff,

"You are all wonderful," he gushed, "Every single one of you, and I am proud of us working so well together to help make this cracking little town a community. As many of you know, I come from London and although I miss the place, I don't think I could ever leave here now."

Somebody booed at this, which elicited a little round of laughter.

"Thank you Bob," Guy continued, "And this year I would like to say a special thank you to a young lady who's giving up her free time to work with us when she can. Madeleine, I'm sure that you have a fantastic career ahead of you. Now without further ado, let's everyone raise our glasses to another successful year."

We all raised our drinks in the air, and Guy motioned to one of the staff to crack open the bottles of champagne. I looked over to see Dave putting his thumbs up to Madeleine, and her standing up. The next thing I knew, she was banging on her glass with a spoon and the room was cast into silence again as everybody looked expectantly over at her.

What was she up to? I remember thinking that she must be really drunk.

"Thank you Guy, for that special mention," she slurred, "And I would like to thank you too for giving me so much time and attention."

Guy beamed.

"You've been particularly attentive to my breasts."

Somebody spluttered.

"Which is lovely," Madeleine continued, "But don't think you've got a chance with me you fat old... Let go, what are you doing?"

Simon had luckily had the good sense to try and shut Madeleine up, and was ushering her away, out of the door, before she knew what was going on.

The room had gone quiet but I could see Dave smirking away and I felt really annoyed with him. I looked to Guy, who had moved to the bar with his back to the room as people started to talk quietly between themselves again, in hushed, uncomfortable tones.

Not wanting to see Guy standing there alone and embarrassed, I walked over to him.

"Guy," I said, touching his arm, "Don't pay any attention to her. Nobody else is. She's just drunk. And a kid still, really. And an idiot."

"Oh that's right," Guy replied with a venom which shocked me, "Blame Madeleine. Do you think I don't know it's what you all think of me? You've probably been winding her up to do this, you and Sheila."

I didn't know what to say and just looked at him.

"See, you're not denying it, are you? No, I know quite well who to blame for this, thank you. Well you've succeeded in making me look like a twat in front of everyone so thanks very much, Jamie."

With that, Guy fled the room and I stood where I was for a moment, scarcely able to believe what had just happened.

After that, the room soon cleared, and I noticed Dave had gone missing again. I went outside for a moment to look for him, and was greeted by the smell of fresh, warm sick from the alleyway down the side of the pub, and the sound of retching. I didn't really want to look but I heard Dave's voice and sure enough, there he was, leaning against the wall while Madeleine was bent over, throwing up, with Simon holding the hair out of her face.

"Oh," I said, wittily, "Ah. Erm, everything OK?"

Madeleine couldn't look up but Simon replied,

"All under control, Jamie, don't worry. I'll take Madeleine back home."

He looked at Dave, "Hadn't you better go back in, mate? Help Jamie sort things out?"

Dave shrugged and then came towards me. I didn't want to look at him. I couldn't help feeling he had some part in this disaster.

"Thanks Simon," I said, "You're a star. Are you sure it's no trouble?"

"It's fine," he said, "No problem at all."

"*Thanks Simon, you're a star*," Dave imitated my words childishly as we returned to the pub.

"Oh just shut up," I said, storming in ahead of him. Perhaps it had been better when I didn't have a partner to bring to these things.

Needless to say, I am not particularly relishing the idea of the next party but if Guy could do it, so could I. He had never mentioned again what had happened, being the type of person who prefers to brush things under the carpet. Madeleine has continued to work with us through her holidays and has also failed to mention that night. Everyone basically ignores the embarrassment, as if doing so means it never happened.

Dave had apologised to me the next day and all was quickly forgotten, until now when I remember thinking I wished I hadn't had a partner. Now of course I regret thinking that way and would give anything for Dave to be with me again, for the events of these last few months never to have happened.

"Will Madeleine be coming to the party?" Brian asks Guy and Sheila nudges him.

"No, I think we'll just have permanent staff members this time," Guy responds as though not bothered by Brian's question, "And no partners either. I think that's for the best."

Chapter Fourteen

I like the way that I can go to work and it feels as though people have forgotten about Dave. I know they haven't but there is a general industriousness about the place which pushes personal matters to one side. This is just what I need right now and, other than Sheila, people generally talk to me about work matters alone, and I am able to get on with my job.

I've just found myself an interesting story actually, which I need to talk to Guy about; I've heard that there's been an application to turn one of the swankier bars in town into a strip club.

I find it hard to think of a worse idea; besides any objection I may have personally, do we really want this place to become a stag do destination? There is a residents meeting about it which I am intending to attend, but I need to get this story authorised. The only problem is Guy.

"Really?" he says when I tell him, looking delighted, "Oh wicked!" Guy has recently started talking like a teenager from the early 1990s.

"Well I don't think so," I tell him, "And not many other people do either, from what I can tell."

"Bunch of old fuddy duddies," he says, "Think of the money that it'll bring to the town."

"Erm, maybe, but do we really want that kind of money?"

"Money's money, Jamie, got to keep the place alive haven't we?"

"I'd say it's doing pretty well as it is actually."

"So, don't tell me, you want to write a disapproving piece of feminist bollocks about why we shouldn't have lapdancing in our pretty little picture postcard town?"

"I want to write a balanced piece about it, about people's feelings and about how this kind of place has affected other towns and cities. Did you know that when strip joints have opened up in other areas, the number of incidents of sexual assaults in their local vicinity has increased?"

Guy sighs. "Well go and write me up a brief on what you want to do. We'll take it from there."

I'm not feeling too hopeful about this one; I can imagine Guy's going to want a lot of input into it. I need to make this balance and I know I have to put personal feelings aside, but so does he. I type up a short synopsis for him, print it out and go back to his office.

He's on the phone, leaning back in his swivel chair. He holds his hand up to me, commanding me to wait.

"Ha ha, that's great, Jim," he says, "We'll see you then. Don't suppose you fancy a round of golf afterwards..?"

Guy is quiet as Jim responds, and glances up at me. With his 'nonchalant' expression affixed to his features he says,

"No, no, of course not, some other time."

He looks slightly disappointed but says goodbye and beckons me in.

"That was Jim," he tells me, "He's coming in at the end of the week for that meeting, you know the one we were meant to have in July, when..."

"I remember," I tell him, not wanting him to finish the sentence, "Do you know what it's about?"

"My lips are sealed," he says, but I get the distinct impression he doesn't know himself. He holds his hand out for my document then skim-reads the brief and smirks a little, which annoys me.

"Go on then," he says, "Have a go but I want to see how you're doing."

"No problem, it's going to take a couple of weeks anyway; the residents' meeting isn't till next Thursday."

"I want you to interview a couple of lapdancers too. Get their point of view. I'll come with you in fact." Snort.

"Right," I say, trying to think of a way to get out of that one. I can't imagine anything worse than having Guy drooling all over some eighteen-year-old bimbo while I try to interview her.

"And if you want a punter's point of view, look no further."

"Thanks. I'll bear that in mind."

Strip Club for Town?

Recent rumours that Exeter businessman, Steven Clarke, has submitted an application to open a 'lapdancing' club in town have been confirmed as correct.

Clarke, 43, who owns a chain of clubs throughout the South West, told the *Advertiser*, "Wherever I've opened a club, towns have seen a boost to their economy. You can expect an increase in business conferences, stag dos and even hen dos. This means more business for the hospitality industry and the high street."

Opinions

As always with such a contentious issue, opinion is divided. A residents' meeting was held on Tuesday evening in order for people with an interest to voice their opinions. By and large, there seems more objection to the idea than support, although a small minority of younger (generally male, although not exclusively!) residents appear to be in favour of the idea.

So, what would a strip club mean to our town?

Some say strip clubs are a bit of light-hearted fun, that they are not part of the sex industry and they actually empower women as those who work in them are able to earn good money for essentially very little work.

These people will also argue that it is the men, the customers of the club, who are being manipulated. This may be the case but it is also worth bearing in mind that most strip clubs are owned and run by men. The women who work in the clubs pay these men for the dubious privilege of doing so.

Besides this, is taking your clothes off for money really being empowered?

Crime surveys in other towns where strip clubs have been opened show a worrying increase in incidents of sexual assaults within the local vicinity. Is this an acceptable price to pay for an injection of cash into the town economy?

Dos and Don'ts

There is also an argument that stag dos and hen dos may not make the ideal visitors to a town. Newquay is a case in point, where local residents complain frequently of anti-social and inappropriate behaviour on their streets.

This is quite aside from the question of whether a strip club is setting the kind of example we want for our young people, male or female.

We have until April next year for the case to be made for or against the opening of this club. Whatever your views, be they positive or negative, perhaps it is time to make your voice heard.

**Any views expressed in this article are those of the author and do not necessarily represent those of the *Advertiser* or Avalon Newsgroup **

Chapter Fifteen

I forget about Jim McKay's meeting until Friday morning when Guy gathers us all together and tells us Jim will be here soon so not to go anywhere. Sheila sighs, having made an appointment that she will now have to cancel. Communication isn't Guy's strong point, but you've probably gathered that by now.

At about half past nine, Jim comes in and Guy is by his side immediately, offering him a coffee.

"Er, yeah, OK," says Jim.

"Great. Sheila, get Jim a coffee would you?"

Jim smiles apologetically at Sheila and greets us all individually. This is nice but the cynical side of me tells me it is learnt management behaviour. Sheila brings him a coffee.

"Shall we go into your office, Guy?" he asks, and Guy readily agrees. I see him perching on the edge of his desk so that Jim can have the chair. It's funny how Guy tries really hard to be the Big Man until his boss appears and he is transformed into Fawning Sycophant.

I try to concentrate on my work but can't help sneaking a look at the scene in the office. Jim looks quite serious, I think, and I am sure I see Guy's shoulders droop a little but I can't see his face so can't be sure. After ten minutes or so, both come out of the office, and Guy does his usual hand-clapping to get our attention. Jim looks quite surprised by this but he lets Guy do the talking,

"Right everybody, gather round. We've got some news for you."

The 'we' does not escape my attention; his usual habit of aligning himself with Jim and drawing a line between us and them.

We draw our chairs together and sit before them. The office is too small for meetings really, especially as the staff numbers have doubled from the time the office was leased. There's talk of getting somewhere new in a couple of years when the lease runs out.

"OK, people," says Guy, "I'm afraid you're not going to like this very much."

"Hang on, Guy," Jim interjects, "It's not necessarily bad news."

"Fine," says Guy, looking at us with a knowing smile, now somehow trying to be one of 'us' instead of 'them', "Without further ado, we need you to know that Avalon is looking to merge a number of papers in the South West, and the *Advertiser* is one of them."

I had not been expecting that. Neither had anybody else, judging by the looks on the faces of my colleagues. I catch Brian's eye and he speaks up.

"What does that mean then, Guy?"

"It means, Brian, that our town paper is no more."

"Is that right, Jim?"

Jim had been looking at Guy with little effort to hide his irritation.

"To some extent Guy's right," he says, "The *Advertiser* as you know it will be changing and becoming part of a bigger, broader news service for people in Cornwall."

"What so we're going to have, like, one paper for the whole of Cornwall?"

"Well yes, that's part of it. But we also need to embrace new ways of doing what we do. I know we already have websites but we need to push these forward, go online in a big way. Create a local news service that can be accessed all over the world."

The pedantic side of me wants to ask what the point is of a local news service anywhere that isn't actually local. I keep quiet though.

Jim continues, "It's something the councils are keen on too, it will help promote tourism we hope, and give the South West an international voice. All the nationals have been running online papers for some time and they're proving very successful.

However, unfortunately, in order to do this properly we are going to have to centralise our services."

Centralisation. I've heard that before. Another way of saying 'job cuts'.

"So what does that mean for us?" Jerry voices what we are all thinking.

"It means," says Jim, "That things will be changing, although I can't tell you exactly how yet as we're still in discussions about where the central offices will be."

"And who the staff will be?" Sheila asks.

"Yes, and who the staff will be," Jim looks at us all as he says this, wanting, I think, to be honest. "You're not stupid and these changes do naturally mean there's a chance of job cuts. Lucy from HR will be coming to consult with you all individually at the beginning of next week."

"Consult," Brian scoffs, "That's useful. Why did you want to come and tell us this today when you can't tell us all the answers?"

"Avalon's big on being honest with its people," Jim says, and I can feel the cynicism which fills the air thickly, "I did want to tell you all earlier but with everything that happened in July, it wasn't quite the time and a couple of months' delay hasn't hurt matters."

He looks at me when he mentions July and I feel myself blushing. I imagine Guy's told him all about what's happened with Dave disappearing.

Luckily only Sheila knows the full story of what I've since found out about Dave. I know she won't have told anybody else, as I hate to be talked about and this is such a ridiculous situation I can't help but still feel embarrassed about it, even though it is not my fault.

"I don't want you to worry," he continues, "Though I realise that's easier said than done, but I wanted to tell you as soon as possible."

"I think I'd rather not know," Jerry says, "Till you can tell us what this really means."

I think he's right. This is ridiculous. We now know our jobs are at risk but nothing more than that. We don't know dates, we don't know any details of the new organisation structure – how big it will be, where offices will be based.

All we know is that it's Friday and we can now look forward to a weekend of worrying and then consultation with 'Lucy from HR' who I've never even heard of before. I have an impulse to laugh, though not with any kind of amusement.

Now I know, I know, there are worse things than this. Worse than being taken for an idiot by the boyfriend I trusted. Worse than being under threat of redundancy (I don't even know yet whether I will lose my job), but I can't help feeling that something is conspiring against me right now. I just hope that the old adage about bad things coming in threes is a load of old cobblers.

After work, I go to the White Hart with Sheila, Jerry and Brian. We ask Guy if he wants to come but he declines. I don't think he's decided yet which side he's on. He must make the right choice after all – if he sticks with Jim there's a chance he can rise with him up the greasy ladder of success but what if Jim doesn't want him?

We have quite a few drinks, and can't seem to keep off the subject of what's going on, despite a number of conscious efforts to change the conversation. The thing is, when you've been hit with shocking news like this, you can't really think of much else. For now this has overtaken the Dave thing in my mind, so perhaps it's a blessing in a strange way, but the reality is that we could all potentially lose our jobs and what would that mean?

Most likely it would mean leaving Cornwall, if we wanted to continue our careers in journalism. It's fairly limited down here in that respect and there aren't many other employment options. Brian and Jerry have families to support, Sheila and Dan want to have kids. I don't know if I'm actually in a better situation because there's just me now but I think with self-pity at the end of the night, as we bid our drunken goodbyes and make our separate ways home, that the others are going back to sympathetic, supportive partners, and I am going back to an empty flat. Unless you count the fish.

My eyes fill with thick, drunken tears and I know I am weaving a bit as I walk up the hill. My feet feel leaden and I am aware that I am very tired. The nights have just started to feel cold, and I don't have a jacket with me so I wrap my arms around myself, pulling my cardigan tight.

So focused on walking in a straight line am I that I don't notice the car immediately but I see it slow down as it passes me, then it pulls in just ahead. Suddenly, I am a bit more alert and I wonder what to do. I don't recognise the car and I can't see who's in it.

Should I turn around and walk back down the hill? Ridiculously, the risk of looking strange, turning right back on my tracks like that, prevents me from doing this. Instead, I slow right down, hoping that the car will drive on by. Instead, the driver's door opens. My heart starts to beat double-time.

"Jamie?" I hear, "I thought that was you."

I look up, and see Simon step out of the car. I would never, ever have felt this nervous here before but it seems that although the gang has now dispersed, it's left a little legacy of fear.

"Are you OK?" he asks.

"Yes thank you, I'm fine. Sorry, just had a few drinks." I hiccup.

"So I see," he grins, "Do you want a lift home?"

"Erm, OK, thanks."

He opens the passenger door and lets me in, then shuts it gently. It's warm in his car and I feel my face begin to glow with the sudden change in temperature.

"So, good night then?" he asks.

"It was OK, thanks," I tell him, not wanting to get into the work situation.

"Russell told me about Dave," he says, and I stiffen up. Why's he gone and mentioned that?

"I was sorry to hear about it," he continues.

"Not your fault," I say, and to change the subject I tell him about what's happened at work today.

"That's awful," he says, and I think 'yes, it is awful', and feel tears pricking at my eyes.

"You'll be OK though, Jamie," Simon says, "Surely. You're getting quite a name for yourself, you know. Those articles about the gang were great, and your write up of Jason's work. He was dead chuffed with that."

I am pleased to think of Jason being happy with me.

"Did you know that Elizabeth Andrews has set up a petition against that strip club by the way? Prompted by none other than your article, I believe!"

I had no idea about this. I don't have time to consider it for long though, as my stomach heaves within me like a boat tossed about on a stormy sea. I clasp my hand to my mouth and luckily Simon notices, pulling over straight away. I lean out of the side of his car and throw up. How delightful. Simon looks concerned.

I look a right state, I'm sure. I just hope he doesn't tell Russell about this.

It's only a couple of minutes in the car and then we're at my home. I thank Simon, and get out, hoping he will just go but he stays and watches as I struggle with unlocking my front door. As I finally get inside, I hear his car pull off, then I am stumbling up the stairs, pulling off my clothes as I go so that by the time I reach my room I am in my underwear and socks and I fall onto my bed and under the spell of a heavy, alcoholic stupor.

In the morning I can feel my hangover before I even open my eyes. My mouth tastes foul, and I know that the moment I move my head, it is going to hurt a lot. There is a sense of foreboding deep within me too, and I piece together the events of yesterday, worrying at the thought of what is going on at work and groaning as I remember my journey home.

End of an *Advertiser* Era?

We are sad to announce that the *Advertiser* as you know it will be no more, as of next year. In a bid to move with the times, Avalon Newsgroup have announced that the paper will be merged with other South West papers and that, as a whole, focus will be moving online.

Relevant

Director Jim McKay told the *Advertiser*, "Whilst we are aware that the decision will not be popular with everybody, we hope that with time our readers will see we have made the right decision. By centralising our services we will be able to ensure value for money and keep all of our news service both commercial and relevant in today's fast-moving world."

No date has been set for the changes to take place but we will keep you informed.

Chapter Sixteen

Ever since I really started thinking about these things, I have considered myself to have four cornerstones in life: friends, family, relationship, career. These are the keys to my happiness.

One of these has gone badly wrong for me in the last few months and it is clear from Jim McKay's news that a second is threatening to go the same way.

I'm trying to be logical, sensible, reasonable. Just about possible when it comes to the work situation; after all, who knows how that will turn out? People always talk about viewing things like this as an opportunity, that they happen for a reason.

That's what I'm trying to think but at the same time I know that things don't always work out for everyone. There are unemployed people, homeless people. OK, I know that with my supportive family there is minimal chance that I could ever end up homeless – in that respect I know I am very, very lucky - but still I don't see that I should just expect this to work out well for me. What makes me so special?

I need to start thinking about other options in case the worst happens. I am well aware that this will most likely mean I have to leave Cornwall though, and the thought of that makes me very sad.

Whereas I can make myself think sensibly about work, unfortunately logic and reason don't come into it when it comes to what's happened with Dave. This is one situation that will not be made sense of. What happened to him that day? What's he doing now? He's alive and that is all I know. That and the fact that after our happy few months together – at least I thought they were happy - he wants nothing to do with me.

If there had been some warning, I might find it easier to deal with, but the whole situation is just so weird, and out of the blue. It's beyond me, what must have been going through his head when he decided he wouldn't even get in touch that day to let me know he was alright. Surely with the events in London he must have known

I would be worried. Even if those bombs hadn't gone off, and he had simply disappeared, I would have been worried anyway.

It doesn't sit right that Dave, the boyfriend I thought I knew, would leave me in such a position. If I'm honest, I'm still concerned for him, but there's nothing more I can do.

For Dave holds all the cards now. If he wants to get in touch, he can; he knows where I live, where I work, where my family and friends live. I opened myself to him completely – my life, my heart - and now I've realised he gave me little of himself in return. But he loved me, I'm sure he did – at least sometimes I'm sure. Other times I just think he was having a good laugh at my expense. But I can't have imagined how close we were, or the way he would look at me. He could have been a very good actor I suppose. I just wish I could talk to him. Find out what really happened to him, and what I really meant to him.

I try not to feel sorry for myself but that's easier said than done. Mum, Dad and Mel have been great. Russell's coming home for Christmas, which he swears is nothing to do with me, but I know him better than that. It's a long way back from Australia, not to mention expensive. I can't wait to see him.

Week by week, I am trying to get on as normal again. This weekend I am going to Mel's; she's succeeded in bullying me into it but I fear I'm not going to be very good company.

The sky is nowhere to be seen as I drive across the moors to Mel's, hidden as it is behind a thick, white mist which has crept in from the sea, bringing with it a sharp chill to the air and an almost eerie peace. This is the type of weather that would have seen shipwrecks in years gone by. I think of the tales of smugglers and ship wreckers with a little shiver. This idyllic part of the world has seen some thoroughly gruesome and horrific events. It's something I'd like to research for the *Advertiser* (or whatever its replacement will be) sometime, if I get the chance.

Mel is waiting for me in the doorway of her house, waving madly, and I can't help but smile to see her. I'm happy I've come. In this moment I feel a relief that I will have a break from my own morose company. I pull up at the side of the house and almost before I have pulled the handbrake up, she is opening the car door, dragging me out for a huge hug while her dog Archie dances around us, wanting to be part of the embrace.

Mel is tall and I always feel dwarfed by her, even though at 5'7" I'm not exactly a short-arse. I'm surprised to see her eyes are shiny with tears, which I think are for me.

I remember when, aged 16, I had my heart broken for the first time, by Jason Taylor. Mel had come round to see me with a box of chocolates and when I had cried on her shoulder, she had welled up too, to see me so bereft. I can never forget that genuine feeling she showed then and I know that coming to see her now is the best thing I could possibly have done.

"I don't look that bad, do I?" I ask.

"You don't look bad. You never look bad! You just look… sad."

That sentence nearly starts me off but I am not going to cry now. Instead, I smile as convincingly as I can and crouch down to give Archie a proper fuss. Immediately, he flops onto his back and paws at me to rub his tummy. I see smoke trickling up into the mist from the neat little chimney and I can't think of anywhere I'd rather be than by Mel's kitchen stove.

Inside, Mel puts the kettle on, and I take a seat at the table, Archie plonking himself right on my feet, pushing his nose into my hand. Mel's is a real farmhouse kitchen, the genuine article. It feels old, lived in, and I love to think of the different people who have lived here over the years. I know Mel does most of her writing in here in the winter and I can understand why. In the summer she will sit outside, shaded by her big sun umbrella. It's beautiful here, idyllic even, but I know she finds it lonely too.

Since her mum died, Mel has lived alone here. It's brave of her, I think, but she says she likes the solitude and being surrounded by memories.

I feel bad that I haven't been here sooner. Somehow or other, Mel and I have not been able to coordinate a visit till this point. I have fallen into a routine – work, home, eat, TV, sleep. There is still a tiny, stubborn yet hopeful part of me that wants to be at home as much as I can, 'just in case', though I don't like to admit that to anybody. I know it's stupid.

Mel seems to have been really busy too; I guess with work, but to be honest, selfishly I haven't even asked.

When I got together with Dave, I had wished that Mel would meet someone too so that she would be as happy as me – although I know Mel is far more sensible than me and just takes things in her stride. She has always been cautious where relationships are concerned, and would never get swept up in things the way I did with Dave. I had just felt that if Mel had met someone then everything would have been perfect and of course I would have not felt so guilty about the amount of time I was spending with Dave – time which I would previously have had with Mel.

As I'm thinking this, Mel plonks two big steaming mugs of tea on the table and fetches a tub of home-baked cookies, then sits down opposite me.

"Right then, want to talk about it? About him? I don't mind if you do or you don't."

"I don't know, Mel. I mean, I do of course, but I don't know where to start. I don't know how I feel or even what I should feel. I don't know if I should be unbelievably angry with him, or still worried about him. God, Mel. When they found his stuff and I thought he was lying in that hospital, that was just so awful."

Mel watches me closely, and says nothing. Lets me carry on at my own pace.

"What am I supposed to feel? I don't know. Where is he and why doesn't he want to get in touch? How could he tell the police he didn't want me to know anything about him? I feel like I've done something wrong, but I know I haven't. I just keep thinking something else has happened to him. When he escaped the Tube bombing, did he get caught up in something else? I know I hadn't known him that long in the great scheme of things Mel, but I did know him. Do know him. I'm sure I do. I just think something bad must have happened. Otherwise he would have been in touch with me. He would have come back for God's sake, if he was OK. It's just too cruel otherwise."

"Oh, Jamie, I don't know what to say. I really don't. I feel like all the practical advice in the world can't quite fit this situation and I can only barely imagine what it's like. It must be really weird not knowing."

"I really think that is the worst thing. I'm totally in limbo. I just have to keep doing the same things – work, home, eat, sleep, get up, work, home, eat, sleep. I'm on auto-pilot. I'm so glad I've come here though, Mel. I really am. I'm sorry I've not been much of a friend this last year."

"Oi! What are you talking about?"

"Well I haven't, have I? Since Dave came on the scene, I mean.

We haven't seen each other half so much."

"Don't be ridiculous!" Mel tells me, "We may not have seen each other all the time but you've always kept in touch, phoning me, yakking on about a load of crap as usual. To be honest it's been a relief not to see so much of you."

She grins at me and puts her hand on mine. What have I done to deserve a friend like this?

We chat about Mel's work as we finish our tea, and I don't want to mention what's happening at the *Advertiser*. I would feel like a drama queen somehow, like there's always something going wrong. Besides which, there's a part of me that wants to try and have some fun now, not be thinking about everything that's making me miserable.

We finish our drinks and, wrapping up warmly, go out for a walk. Archie races ahead, vanishing briefly into the mist and then reappearing suddenly from a completely different direction, a big daft grin plastered over his face. We tread carefully over the moorland; with the thick mist around us, it's difficult to make out the terrain. Staying near to the stone wall means we won't get lost but even knowing the place as well as Mel does, there's always a chance of stumbling and twisting an ankle.

I'm struck by the eeriness again, and find my thoughts turning to the people who have been lost up here in years gone by. The tin miners killed by a collapsed mine shaft. I've always thought this is the perfect place for a ghost story; I've suggested it to Mel before but actually I might like to write it myself.

I am pondering this, whether it would be a good way to take my mind off the other events in my life, as we walk, and Mel is presumably wrapped up in her thoughts too. We don't talk for some time and I enjoy the companionable silence and the comfort of just being with my friend. Occasionally one of us will call for Archie if he disappears for too long, but he never strays too far, bounding back up to us with the odd stick he finds, and trying to tempt us to chase him for it. No chance.

The stillness which the mist brings with it is striking; often up here the wind from the sea blows right across, whistling through the sparse trees and hedgerows and battering down the long grasses. Today it is cold and quiet but the murmur of the sea is still there, constant and comforting. Through the mist comes the occasional call of a lonely gull, ghostly and shrill in the quiet.

The kitchen feels so welcoming when we return, and I am drawn immediately to the hearthside where we'd left a bottle of red wine before we went out. I pick it up and raise my eyebrows at Mel.

"I might have one later," Mel says, "I feel a bit dodgy today. Don't let that stop you though!"

She tosses a corkscrew in my direction. It clangs on the stone of the hearth and Archie comes over to sniff at it. While I open the bottle, Mel pours herself a glass of lemonade. I glug some wine into my glass and we toast each other, then both speak at once.

"There's something else," I say.

"There's something I have to tell you," says Mel.

We look at each other, and I laugh. Mel looks a bit uncomfortable, I think. Perhaps she's just had enough of my dramas.

"It's nothing major," I quickly tell her, "Well sort of... it's my job..."

"I know," she interrupts, looking me in the eye.

"You know about the merger? How?"

I can't believe how quickly news gets around the industry, it's frightening.

"Jim told me," says Mel.

I am blank for a moment then think of Guy's boss.

"Jim McKay? Are you working for him? He's such a twat. Coming in, giving us the usual corporate bullshit. Guy absolutely loves him of course."

"I'm not working for him, no."

"Good! I wouldn't bother. He'd probably just sack you halfway through the job anyway."

"I'm seeing him, Jamie."

"You're *what*?"

I look at Mel, unsure if I've heard her correctly. She looks back at me steadily but worriedly. It's not often that Mel looks nervous but she does right now.

"What do you mean, seeing him?" I ask, though I realise it's a stupid question.

"Just that, Jamie. We're having a relationship."

"But, but he's married. With kids." I blurt out, stupidly.

"I know," Mel looks down at the glass in her hands.

"Well is he still with his wife?"

"Yes."

"What... what are you doing? What's going on?"

Mel seems unable to look at me, concentrating instead on the bottle opener she is fiddling with. I stay quiet and she tells me her story.

It turns out Mel and Jim have been seeing each other for nearly a year. They got together just after Dave and I did, at a conference in London.

They've known each other a few years of course – the world of journalism isn't that big, especially in the West Country – Mel had actually heard about the opening for my job through Jim. Does she expect me to be grateful for that now?

"I wasn't with him then though, Jamie. We just got on really well. I just, I don't know, this just happened. I know how it must sound, how I must look. How he must look. He loves his wife and kids, he really does, but he and Angela are more like... more like friends."

"Right. And I guess she doesn't understand him."

"Don't be like that, Jamie. Jim's not like that."

I raise my eyebrows but Mel ignores me and carries on with her story.

Apparently she has always liked Jim but, she says, would never have acted on it and just put any thought of it out of her head. It was just one of those things. A couple of years back she'd done quite a bit of work for one of Avalon's magazines and in doing so had started to see more and more of Jim. They had clicked, she said, always had a great laugh together and she found him really easy to talk to. Over time she'd come to think about him an awful lot and had started to realise that perhaps he liked her too, but she had tried to push all those thoughts out of her head. Inevitably it was drink that had provided the catalyst and at some convention or other, they had sat together at dinner, drunk quite a lot between them, and sat up chatting all night. Just chatting, Mel insists, until the early hours of the morning when they went to bed (separately) but kissed in the lift. She had tried to forget about it, he had too, but they had been drawn back together and in time were in the grips of an all-consuming affair.

No wonder she didn't mind that we'd not seen much of each other this last year, I think to myself grimly. She'd probably been glad that I was spending so much time with Dave – it made keeping her little secret easier.

"So what are you going to do?" I ask.

"I don't know, I don't know, Jamie. Don't be angry at me."

I am though. Angrier than I want to be, but I am trying not to show it. I try to question myself; am I allowed to feel angry? Is it any of my business? What is it with people, though? How can they not care about others' feelings?

I want to shake her. I just grip my wine glass. Slowly, thoughts swirl in my mind and begin to click together.

I remember Mel somehow knew Dave was in London on the day of the bombs. Jim had heard from Guy... he must have told Mel. That was why she phoned me, concerned.

"So why are you only telling me this now?" I ask, "I'm meant to be your best friend, Mel."

"I know, I'm sorry, Jamie, it's complicated though isn't it? With the work situation and everything."

"I hardly ever see Jim, though," I say, "It's not like I'd say anything to him. Surely you know me better than that, Mel."

"I mean your work situation," she says quietly, "The merger."

"Well that's only just happening now, and you've had over a year to tell me about Jim."

I look at her and she doesn't meet my eye.

"Oh." I say.

"I'm sorry, Jamie, I'm really sorry. I couldn't say anything though. How could I?"

"How could you not, more like?" I explode, "I don't believe this, Mel. How long have you known my job's been at risk? I can't believe you haven't told me. How could you choose to keep loyal to some cheating, smarmy bastard who won't even leave his wife for you?"

"Jamie..."

"What? What are you going to say? You know how much I love that job. Thanks Mel, thanks very much."

I bang my glass down on the table and stand up. Archie jumps, startled awake from his dream, looking bewildered.

"Jamie, you said it yourself, you've been caught up in the whole Dave thing."

"Right, so now you throw that back in my face as well. Thanks again, you really are a fantastic friend."

"I don't mean, I didn't mean... Jamie, sit down, please."

"Why?"

"Because you're my best friend. Because this hasn't been easy for me."

"Ahh, poor Mel. It must have been awful."

"It has actually, I've hated it. But I couldn't tell you. Jim shouldn't have told me. Imagine what a mess it would have been if all of that came out."

"Right. Well at least I know where I stand anyway. Thanks, Mel. See you later."

I push back my chair and grab my bag, then leave the cosy kitchen to a shock of cold air and drive home.

Visibility is poor. I find myself engulfed in clouds of mist, which my headlights are barely able to penetrate.

I know I've had a glass of wine and I'm in a frenzied emotional state. I probably shouldn't be driving back right now, up here on the moors all alone, but I'm not stupid. Naive, maybe. Gullible? It certainly seems that way; but not stupid. I take my time, I know the roads, and I get home safely.

Back in my flat again, I go upstairs and once more I fall onto my bed, upset. This is becoming a habit.

So much for those four cornerstones of my life. Interesting how crumbly and unstable three of them have turned out to be. All I need now is for my family to disown me and I've got the full hand.

Chapter Seventeen

Christmas. I am trying not to compare it to last year but how can I not? Twelve months ago, Dave had been living with me for a matter of weeks. We had a lazy morning in bed, drinking coffee and opening presents, before walking through town to have lunch with my parents. I wonder if Dave is thinking of this too? Wherever he is, whoever he's with. I just can't believe that he's screwed up all our shared experiences, our memories, and chucked them away like rubbish.

Last Christmas was a crisp, cold day and the winter sun scattering sparkles generously, all over the vast sea. This year it is damp and grey. Not cold, not warm. It's not even raining. It just is.

I try not to let my family know how I feel. After all, Russell has come back from his travels (for me?), and Mum and Dad are trying to make it a happy day. I haven't told my family about what's happened with Mel, although it must be obvious that something is up. If they mention her I just change the subject, but despite my anger at her, I still feel some loyalty and I don't want them thinking badly of her as well. I think this is something I have to work out myself, and have no intention of turning other people against her.

I stayed at Mum and Dad's last night, and we all went to Midnight Mass. We walked to the church and, despite everything, I felt the unmistakeably warm Christmas cheer seeping into me. I do love the streets here at Christmas; strings of lights criss-cross above shoppers' heads and each shop has a small Christmas tree lit up above its doorway. The church tower hosts an enormous star which glows above the rooftops and casts a little Christmas magic over the town.

Russell met us at church after a few drinks with his mates but I opted to stay in with Mum and Dad.

Sam, beautiful old dog, was out for the count when we left the house, snoring and contented. In former times he would have been at the door, watching us go, feeling sorry for himself. Now he's older I think he is just glad of the rest. Earlier in the evening I was even able to brush out his fur while he slept – clumps of old, matted, greying hair came away in my hand. He used to hate being groomed, trying to wrestle the brush from my hand with his mouth. This time he was tucked so deeply into his sleep that I don't think he even knew I was there, but the result is a smarter-looking dog, more like his old self.

This morning I got up to find a stocking had been left out for me, and one for Russell. Lots of silly gifts, and small chocolate treats, were stuffed inside. It's been years since we had stockings at Christmas, and I fight the urge to feel sad at the thought of childhoods lost. Mum and Dad are trying to make us happy after all; it would be pretty churlish of me to turn it into something sad.

We've had drinks at regular intervals since the bucks fizz at breakfast, the result of which is that we don't get round to dinner till way into the afternoon and afterwards we all sit around feeling extremely over-full. Even though it's not that cold, there is a fire burning in the hearth as it would break with tradition not to have one.

In the warm, sunny room, Dad dozes for a while and Mum, Russell and I flick through our respective books. My main present this year is from all three of them – a new laptop. A far bigger present than we normally give each other, and the CDs and books I have chosen for them pale in comparison.

They tell me they want me to write again, outside work. To write for the love of it like I used to, so that it doesn't get mixed up with the feelings I have about my job.

I love it, and the way I feel an unexpected flicker of excitement at the thought of writing. Maybe this year I will write my book. Maybe the misery I've been feeling will bring out my most creative side.

We watch re-runs of *Only Fools and Horses* on one of the cable channels and pick at various different nibbles (even though I don't think any of us actually wants to eat anything), finishing the day with a couple of games of cards and a nightcap. None of us makes it up past eleven and when I go to bed I give each of my family a big hug and a kiss to say thank you, although Russell says 'urgh' and pushes me away. Nothing like Christmas to bring out the child in you again.

In my childhood bedroom I gaze up at those faded stars and I feel quite content – more than I have for some time. I thank God, whoever or whatever that is, for my family. I know, without a doubt, that they will never, ever let me down. I can't help but be grateful for that.

I go back to my flat on Boxing Day and I set up my new laptop. In the hallway I clear the small, scratched table which will have to act as a desk for now, and I fiddle about with the settings on the computer, then get distracted by playing about on the Internet.

I want to write but I sit there blankly, typing a few lame sentences and deleting them. I end up feeling really annoyed with myself and decide to go out for a walk. It is a slightly nicer day than its predecessor and there are loads of people out, walking off their Christmas excesses, letting the restorative wind from across the sea blow away the feelings of over-indulgence and guilt. Not many people out walking on their own, I think, and then I'm annoyed at myself once more for my self-pity.

When I return to the flat I knock on Mrs Butters' door but there's no answer. She's probably still at Caroline's. I am glad really, as I think some time to myself is what I need now. It also means I can put on my music as loud as I want, without bothering her. I go up to my flat and pour myself a glass of wine, glance at the parcel addressed to me in Mel's writing, and put it into one of the top cupboards.

I still can't bear to think about my supposed best friend. Although I don't hate her, I can't shake this anger. I am self-aware enough to realise that some of this anger is very probably being redirected from the absent Dave, and from my employers. However, I still can't believe she kept quiet all that time about Jim, or the fact that I might be losing my job. Where does her loyalty lie? Not with me, it appears.

Switching on my new laptop, I open the window slightly although it is far from warm outside. I just want to keep breathing in the fresh Cornish air. I need its energy.

This time when I start to write I don't look back at the previous sentences. I am not writing anything structured, I am just writing. Letting it all out. Anger, sadness, bitterness, self-pity, guilt, anything and everything. It is safe here on my computer and nobody else need ever see it. It's nearly three hours later that I feel spent and I save the document into a new folder I call 'Private' – even though if anybody ever feels the urge to nose about in my hard drive, surely this name will actually make this the first folder they want to look into?

I open up the Internet and check my emails. I lazily look at YouTube in case something funny catches my eye. I am then tempted by one of my bad habits – type in Dave's name to the search engines and see what comes up. I have never found anything of interest. It's not as if he has an unusual name. I don't even know what I'm looking for. Today though I stop myself, and instead I switch the machine off. I make an early resolution for 2006 – it's time to move on. It may be easier said than done but if I don't try I will never know.

On New Year's Eve, Russell persuades me to come out with him and his friends. I don't know that I want to really but he gives me such a hard time that in the end it's easier to say yes.

He doesn't mention Mel, which I know is a carefully deliberate omission but I'm glad of it. Our little gang consists of Cara and Amy, both of whom Russell had gone out with whilst at school (though at different times, I hasten to add), Simon (who also went out with Amy at school, though at a different time to Russell), Alan (who went out with Cara... it's a small town, OK?), and Harry (who is gay and subsequently went out with nobody whilst at school).

This group of friends had all been in the same school year and only Simon still lives here; all the others live and work in London. It is good to see them all and I'm starting to think that a night out isn't such a bad idea. In fact, if I'm not much mistaken, I may actually be looking forward to it.

I don't know if you will have spent a New Year's Eve in a Cornish town but for many it is tradition that everybody goes out in fancy dress. Our town is no exception and is in fact renowned for its celebrations. There was some worry last year, what with the gang and all the trouble they'd been causing, but nothing happened. They would have been overwhelmed by the sheer volume of people, plus I suppose they wouldn't have known who they could pick on, as everybody is dressed up.

I'm not a big one for fancy dress usually but I will make an exception for New Year's. It makes for a really friendly atmosphere, helped by the huge influx of visitors and also the fact that everybody is hidden away in their disguises. Perhaps a little to do with the vast quantities of booze which are consumed as well.

Earlier in the day, Cara and Amy convinced me to dress up as the third of the Three Bears, as Alan is dressed as a six-foot-something Goldilocks, complete with fake bosom and a blonde nylon wig that must surely be a fire hazard. Russell, Simon and Harry are the Three Musketeers.

As we make our way down the side streets, I can't help but get caught up in the excitement and for the first time in ages I really do feel in high spirits. From the top of the town we can hear the music coming from the harbourside. There's always a DJ and sound system, playing suitably cheesy music throughout the night. Amy is carrying a rucksack filled with bottles of ready-mixed gin and tonic, plus a bottle of Cava for midnight itself.

On reaching the town I smile to see it so transformed, with people spilling out of the pubs and flooding the streets, trickling onto the harbour beach and dancing under the street lamps. Amongst the crowds I can make out a group of cowboys and Indians accompanied by a pantomime horse, and a flock of about thirty bishops. There are children dressed like Bob the Builder, men dressed like women, and women dressed like men. Princess Leia, Darth Maul, pirates and Teenage Mutant Ninja Turtles.

We decide it's not worth trying to get into the pubs and instead head straight for the harbour beach, where we sit on the wall and pass the bottles of gin and tonic along the line and back again. People stop to chat or take our pictures. Many people here will be tourists, in town for the party, but it's hard to tell who is who.

The hours leading up to midnight pass in a very pleasant blur. The sounds of Europe's *The Final Countdown* begin to boom out of the PA, and Cara pops open the bottle of Cava. At midnight there is cheering everywhere, and hugs from friends and strangers. Thoughts of Mel and of Dave cross my mind - I wonder what they're doing now – but I don't have time to think as somebody taps me on the shoulder and, before I know it, I have been dragged into a huge conga, snaking its way around the harbour beach and back down again. I can't help but laugh.

When I return, hoping that the others are still there, I see Russell, who hugs me and dances me around.

"Happy New Year, little sis," he says with a definite slur in his voice, then before I know it he has turned away and is kissing Cara quite passionately. *Interesting*, I think. I hope they're not going to regret this.

I look around for the rest of our group. Goldilocks appears to be getting off with Catwoman but I spot Amy and Simon laughing together a few metres away, sitting on the wall and opening a bottle of sambuca. Am I going to be a gooseberry if I join them? Suddenly I'm aware of a little wave of self-pity within me, at the thought of all these happy people, couples, families.

Last year I was here on this very beach with Dave, Mel and a few of our friends from school. Luckily Simon sees me before I have too much time to dwell on this, and he calls me over. Amy passes me the bottle of sambuca and although I know I probably shouldn't, I do.

Before long, the three of us are walking away from the centre of town, knocking mouthfuls of the sweet spirit back and singing Bohemian Rhapsody at the top of our voices, then collapsing into helpless, breathless laughter.

We head out of town up to St Nicholas' Chapel, disturbing the poor old gulls who have gathered here for the night, away from the crowds down below. They rise together, white ghosts, glowing against the dark backdrop of the night time sea.

It's windy up here, with the sea on three sides of us. My cheeks are stinging a little and tears spring up in my eyes, from the cold blasts, but it feels good.

We find a bench and sit down, Simon between me and Amy with one arm around each of us. From here we can look back to town, or out into the deep inky blackness, where the odd distant light can be seen bumping up and down on the waves, and the lighthouse across the bay flashes its dependable message of warning.

Away from the crowds and the PA, after New Year has been rung in and the corks have popped, it feels like we have run out of things to say. I am happy to be quiet for a moment, to contemplate the last year, which has been undoubtedly the most crazy of my life to this point. However, I start to wonder again if I actually am interrupting things between Simon and Amy; trying to work out if I should make my excuses and just go.

Suddenly, Amy springs up and leans over the wall, and before I know it she is throwing up. Simon is by her side, holding her hair back, and I am reminded of him doing this same thing for Madeleine.

"You're very good at that," I say, but I don't think he hears me. He rubs Amy's back and when she has finished he sits her down again then says we will walk her home.

The three of us set off once more, with no singing this time; not even any talking in fact. I hear my breath labouring as we take the steep hill to Amy's house. By now I am shattered. She manages to unlock her front door and hug us both, whispering to us very loudly that she needs to be quiet as her dad will be in bed. As it happens, he's not. He comes through, takes one look at his daughter with her slightly stained bear costume, raises an eyebrow at Simon and me and tells us he will take it from here. He thanks us for bringing Amy home, wishes us a happy New Year then closes the door.

And then there were two.

I wonder if we should try and find the others but decide against it. Who knows where they are, or what they're doing?

"Right," I say to Simon, "I guess that's New Year's then."

"Guess so," he says, "Unless you fancy another drink somewhere?"

Amy's throwing up has thoroughly put me off even another drop of alcohol. Contemplating the hangover I might expect in the morning, I politely say no thank you. I think Simon is relieved too.

"How are you getting home? " I ask him; his farm's a few miles out of town.

"Think I'll be walking... I'll walk you back first though."

"You don' t have to do that," I weakly protest, but I would be glad of his company and I can't deny that I feel a bit more nervous walking on my own in the dark nowadays.

At my front door, I ask if he wants a coffee but Simon is keen to get going as he will have to be back on the farm in time for his chores. I don't suppose he will have a chance to sleep at all tonight. I hug him and wish him a happy 2006, then watch as he walks off up the hill.

All is dark in the house; Mrs Butters will long have been asleep. I climb wearily up the stairs and switch on the kettle. I'll have a hot chocolate in bed then drift off to sleep.

When I wake up it will be a new year and, although I'm not really feeling that optimistic, who knows what it will bring?

Happy New Year!

The staff at the Advertiser would like to wish you all a very happy 2006; the last year that the Advertiser will be in its present format.

The town once again saw record numbers of visitors flooding in to enjoy the celebrations which were even bigger and better than last year.

Bishops

Tony Mahoney, local DJ, kept the crowds entertained with his selection of fine tunes, well into the small hours of the morning. The majority of partygoers were in fancy dress as usual, with notable examples including thirty bishops, and the usual crew of Elvises (Ed's note: should this be Elvii?!).

There were no arrests made and police Sgt Tom Merritt told the *Advertiser*, "We are delighted that once again this busy night saw little or no trouble and residents and tourists were able to enjoy an exciting and happy event."

Chapter Eighteen

I'm glad of the new year, even though nothing has really changed that much.

At work, we have a new boss, who is sort of between Jim and Guy. Her name is Valerie Simpson and she seems quite nice. She is a 'media management consultant' apparently and she does enjoy a bit of name dropping ("When I worked with Piers..." – Jerry chooses to ignore the reference to Piers Morgan and asks instead if it was the Clevedon and Weston piers. Valerie is not amused).

She has previously worked at the *Daily Mail*, but I try not to hold this against her. She has been brought in to see the merger through. She is obviously very experienced and I hope she'll help Jim and his fellow directors make the right decisions, though I am a little worried that she is an 'outsider', as how can she really know any of our papers (or any of us) well enough?

I'm not sure Guy's too happy about her being here, but in the current climate he can't afford to do anything but practise his already finely honed sucking-up skills.

He makes a big deal about the upcoming *Advertiser* party which is at the end of the week, and insists that she come to it.

He doesn't employ the 'work hard, play hard' line which he always hits one of us with if we don't fancy a night out – personally I'm not convinced that applying pressure to people is conducive to their having fun – however, he makes it impossible for her to say no.

"Oh, erm, I don't think I can, Guy."

"What's wrong, Valerie? Not good enough for you?" Snort.

"No, no, of course not, it's just I'm..."

"Now don't tell me you're busy, I heard you telling Jim you had no plans this weekend! Come on, if you're really committed, you'll come! That is, unless you really do think we're beneath you!" Snort.

I sneak a look at Valerie and see her flushed face. She is inwardly fuming, I can see, but she fronts a smile and says sweetly, "Of course

I'll be there, Guy, I wouldn't miss it!"

I think Guy wants to show her what a great job he's done and how wonderful his townsfolk think he is. It's just a good job she didn't come to last year's nightmare event, I think.

Valerie begins her new job by spending some time with each of us, accompanying us to any interviews and looking through our past work. She is full of questions and, although I start off determined to be fairly reticent in what I disclose to her, I find myself opening up. I surprise myself by talking quite passionately and openly about what I think of the paper, the environment we work in; even the sexism which has coloured my working life so far.

I am not trying to affect her view about any of my colleagues but I enjoy being able to express my opinions openly, to somebody who seems to want to listen. I'm not sure she understands all that I say but the main thing is she has shown an interest. It also makes a refreshing change to have a female in charge.

Sheila doesn't take to Valerie though; "I just don't trust her," she says. "Not totally sure why. Don't you think she's just a bit too... *interested* though? Don't say too much to her, Jamie, not till you're really sure you can trust her."

"Oh I don't know, Sheila, not everybody's out to get us. If she can see how things really are, she'll see who's good at their job, surely?"

"Hmm, well I'm not about to give too much away."

Sheila leaves it at that but I think she is over-reacting a bit. At least now Valerie's here, there are no more overtly sexist or sexual comments in the office. I think our new boss has the men running scared. I quite like it.

On the day of the *Advertiser* party, Valerie is not in the office as she has agreed to come along that evening so she's working from home during the day.

There is muttering about this, largely from Guy and Brian, but I think it's fair enough seeing as she lives up in Somerset and the party's being held on a Friday night. She already spends enough time away from home as it is, though I'm guessing she's very well recompensed for this.

As it turns out, I'm kind of glad she's not there. In the early afternoon I receive a phone call from Mum, telling me some news we've been expecting for some time. Our lovely Sam is ill, and the vet doesn't think anything more can be done for him.

I take the news matter-of-factly. I am at work, after all, but I know I can't just sit here now and deal with it. I go and explain to Guy who, although he may not be a big animal lover and possibly has no idea why I would want to, agrees to let me go and see my dog for the last time. I say it is for my parents too, and of course it is, but I really don't want to miss this opportunity to say goodbye to our faithful, loving dog.

I have a feeling Valerie would frown upon this kind of thing. She definitely doesn't strike me as an animal lover and I suspect would see this as a weakness. I guess she's had to be very strong to get where she is. However, even if she were here I think I would have to insist on going. Some things are just more important.

I race up the hill to Mum and Dad's, hoping I don't see anybody I know. When I get there, Mum lets me in and tells me Dad is upstairs. Sam is in his favourite place, lying on the lounge carpet over the bit of floor which houses the hot water pipes. He cottoned onto this very soon after coming to us as a tiny pup, and claimed it as his own place. He is breathing shallowly, but appears to be fast asleep.

I sit on the floor next to him, as gently as I can, but I wake him anyway and as he opens his eyes to look at me he wags his tail ever so slightly. His eyes look sad, and tired, and I feel my own now fill with tears. There is no holding them back any longer and I let them plop fatly to the floor and into Sam's fur as I put my face close to his and tell him I love him.

I am quite aware that to some people this is madness, he is just an animal, but I think you know me well enough by now to understand that I don't believe there is any such thing as 'just an animal'.

Sam, to me, is especially important. He cured me of my fear of dogs, in fact turned that around completely so that I am now convinced they are one of the best things in the world. He has been by my side, and Mum's, Dad's and Russell's, for over sixteen years. We've watched him grow from a tiny, cute pup through his troublesome, long-limbed maniac stage, into a (fairly) well-behaved, affectionate adult dog.

I have so many memories of him; his absolute ecstasy at his first experience of snow and the way his hot tongue licked my cold hands to warm them up; the many times we have run and played on the beach together, him barking and bothering me to throw more stones, more sticks, so that he would chase them into the sea, shaking his head to clear it of the water and bounding up to me, shaking his wet fur and soaking me; times when I was growing up, of feeling he was the only one I could trust – hugging him to my self-pitying teenage form and him patiently sitting with me for as long as I wanted.

Now he's come to the end, and I am sure he's had a good life. I am sure he's been happy. The trouble with pets is they will never, or rarely, be with us to the end. That's the nature of it all but knowing that doesn't really make it any easier.

Mum comes over and touches my head.

"How's Dad?" I ask.

"Not great, you know what he's like about the dog."

Mum's eyes turn to Sam, and are filled with sadness too. She always calls him 'the dog' but she loves him as much as any of us do. She, in fact, has spent the most time with him – the pair of them in and around the house while Dad was at work and Russell and I were at school, then college, then university.

"So is it definite?" I ask.

"I'm afraid so, Jamie. We're to take him in about half an hour. I'm glad you've had a chance to see him though."

I hear Dad coming downstairs and determine to be brave for him. He comes into the room looking ashen-faced.

"Hi Dad," I say, "Are you OK?"

"I'm alright, sweetheart," he tells me, stooping to kiss my head, "Come to say bye, have you?"

"I have," I lift Sam's head gently so he wakes again, and looks at me through those big brown eyes. They are rimmed with red and I can see he's exhausted. Still, it's a difficult decision to end his life. How do we ever know that's the right thing to do?

In Sam's case, his age and ill health have put an end to all the things he's enjoyed in life, and left him unable to cope on his own. In the wild, animals would crawl off or be picked off, in this weakened state. Although Sam is a domesticated animal and therefore the same rules don't necessarily apply, I don't think he can ever be happy again. In fact Mum has told me he was quite distressed earlier at not being able to get outside, and making a mess on the kitchen floor. His legs just won't carry him and he needs to be helped to his feet just to stand.

I don't know how I can leave him but I have to. Mum and Dad need to get going to the vets and I still have this stupid party to go to, which really is an even more unappealing prospect now.

I lean my head onto Sam's, feeling that familiar bony lump on the top of his skull, hearing his breath as he sighs into me.

"I love you, Sam," I whisper to him.

I don't suppose he understands, but I hope he can feel it all the same. He puts his head back on his paws and his eyes close once more.

I get up and tell Mum and Dad that I hope it goes OK. My voice falters. I have to rush from the house and round the corner, where I lean on a wall and let the tears come.

I don't care who sees me now; what does it matter?

Chapter Nineteen

Needless to say, I am not in any mood for the work party that night. After my tears have subsided, I walk dejectedly back to the flat, where Mrs Butters is out in the front garden, filling up her bird feeder. She looks up at me as I come in, and asks if I'm alright. I tell her what's happened.

"Oh I'm sorry, Jamie," she tells me, "I don't know what I'd do if I lost Charlie."

"Thanks Mrs Butters," I say, "I know. Sam was old though, I guess he's had enough now."

I think of him; has it happened yet? How are Mum and Dad? I also realise that what I've just said may not be particularly sensitive towards somebody who is quite old herself.

"I know the feeling!" she jokes.

"I've got to go to the *Advertiser* party tonight as well," I say, "Just to top it all off!"

I brave a smile at her and head indoors. I need a hot bath and a cup of tea, then to paint a face on and just get through the night.

Don't drink too much, I tell myself repeatedly, for fear of breaking down. It feels like any number of things could tip me over the edge tonight. Thinking about Sam. Remembering our last work party, or just the fact that my boyfriend's gone, inexplicably; or that I've fallen out with my best mate. Oh, and let's not forget that I might lose my job. Take your pick.

Dan is giving Sheila a lift and they pick me up on the way. I'm glad to have somebody to arrive with.

"I see the old witch is here already," whispers Sheila, spying Valerie across the room.

Our new boss is dressed in a bright blue jacket with shoulder pads, and trousers with high heels, like a parody of a power-dressing Eighties woman, only I know this is no parody. You can't have everything I suppose. It seems she is one of those people who is

118

stuck in that decade, doomed forever to frosted pink lipstick and pale blue eyeshadow.

I watch as she works the room though, unhindered by her ill-advised fashion choices, talking to the guests, taking an interest in them. She seems to ooze a natural ease and charm. No wonder she's done so well for herself.

It's the same venue as last year – The White Hart – and I do think I see a look of mild distaste on Valerie's face. Even though to my eyes, she and this function room could have been made for one another, she evidently thinks she is a bit above all of this. To be fair though, I suppose that makes it more in her favour that she's deigned to join us.

It's the same crowd as last year except that none of the staff have brought partners. And there is no Madeleine.

Simon has turned up again, and he's brought Jason, the youth worker from St Austell. It's good to see them both and I surprise myself for feeling a little bit cheered (maybe even a bit excited?) by their presence. Well I suppose there's no getting round the fact of Jason's very fine eyes.

I don't want to tell Simon about Sam, even though he was the offspring of Simon's own dogs and I know Simon will be sympathetic. I don't think I could get the words out now without showing myself up.

"How are Vanessa and Anthony?" I ask Jason, and he tells me Vanessa is still working at the farm but Anthony's moved up to Bristol where he's helping out at his cousin's music studio.

Simon tells me with a big grin that his dad is loads better than he was, but that he's decided Simon needs to be dealing with these tedious social events as he's got more time to waste. Simon is clearly relieved that his dad's on the mend and I wonder if this means he'll be able to leave the farm again. Would he want to, I wonder?

I leave them both at the bar and promise to come back later. For now there is socialising to be done and I'm keen to prove to the world, and myself, that I'm doing OK.

Valerie catches up with me during the evening, and buys me a large glass of wine.

"Take the weight off your feet for a bit, Jamie," she tells me, and I wonder if I am paranoid or whether she really did cast her eye over my less-than-flat stomach as she said it. "Come and sit down and have a chat."

As we take a seat, I notice her casting a glance Guy's way. He is currently laughing loudly (no doubt at one of his own jokes) with Bill Turner from the Red Bull.

"So how are you, Jamie?"

Her face is a picture of concern. Something about it puts me on edge.

"I'm fine thank you, Valerie."

"Good. I must say you look very well, but this business with your young man must have been quite unsettling."

I feel myself close up, my hackles rise. What does she know about Dave? Who's been talking? Again she glances at Guy, and I wonder if it was him. Of course, I think, he's probably been spilling all our secrets, trying to ingratiate himself with her. I look at the woman sitting in front of me, who I have been fairly candid with since she joined us, and wonder how I could have been so stupid. She looks back calmly at me, her head tilted ever-so-slightly to one side, the very picture of concern.

"Er, yep. Don't really want to talk about it though, thanks all the same."

"Sure, sure," she says soothingly, her voice thickly, sickly honeyed, "I understand. It must have been a bad time for you lately. I can understand how you might not be able to concentrate on your work sometimes."

Oh God, I think, what is she saying? Is she implying I am not up to my job? I suddenly understand what people mean when they say the scales have fallen from their eyes. Sheila was right. Why did I not spot this straight off? I think I was too busy hoping we'd got somebody sensible at last. Valerie seems altogether too keen, though, to root out people's weak points.

"Tell me more about Guy then," she says.

"Guy?"

"Yes, you know, the fat tosser over there. Your boss."

I'm quite shocked by this; I'd taken her to be a professional person. Of course Guy's a tosser, it's obvious to anyone, but also correctly he is my boss and I don't think she should be talking about him like this to me.

"Well what about him?"

"Do you think he should keep his job?"

"He's fine." I say.

"Oh come on, you can tell me, he's not exactly forward-thinking, is he? You've said as much yourself. I've heard all about him spending work time on eBay and organising his social life, too."

"I... what do you want me to say, Valerie? I don't think this is a particularly appropriate conversation."

"It's just between you and me, I promise," she says, "You want me to make the right choices when it comes to this merger, don't you?"

What is that supposed to mean? Is it a threat? She looks at me innocently, but my suspicions are raised now and I want to get out of this conversation. Has Jim put her up to this, I wonder? I wouldn't put it past the cheating scumbag, I think. But an image of Mel pops into my head and I just can't quite believe she would be with someone who was such a total bastard. Would she? People do lose their heads when it comes to love – look at me.

Shit, I think, maybe it was Jim who's told Valerie about Dave. I bet he knows everything about me, thanks to Mel. Brilliant.

"Of course I do," I play dumb, "You probably need to spend a bit more time with us all, I guess, and come to your own conclusions. Now if you'll excuse me, I need to go and speak to those gentlemen over there."

I take my glass and wander over to Simon and Jason, wondering if I should tell Sheila about the conversation I've just had. The two men smile at me.

"I've just been talking to Simon about Ivy House," Jason tells me.

"Oh yes?" I say, my mind still on Valerie. I'm trying to remember what I've said to her over the last couple of weeks. Have I let my defences down too much? Almost certainly. Will it be used against me? Who knows?

Simon's been saying something to me. I pick up on him mentioning the boy who attacked Mrs Butters, whose trial is scheduled in the spring. He and Jason are looking at me for a response.

"I hope they lock him up and throw away the key," I say venomously, and notice the surprise on my companions' faces.

"Oh not really," I say, "I know that won't solve anything. He can't just get away with it though."

I explain to Jason that Mrs Butters is my neighbour so I do have some personal interest in the case.

"Don't you think though, maybe if this kid had been picked up earlier and given something else to do with his time, this might have been prevented?" Jason asks.

"Erm, yeah, sure, I guess so."

I'm watching Valerie, talking to Brian. They seem deep in conversation. Simon and Jason are looking at me once more.

"Oh I'm sorry, ignore me, I've just got a lot on my mind. I'll come and see you again in a bit."

I know I ought to tell Guy that Valerie's got it in for him but after last year's little drama I don't think this is the time or place. I look for Sheila, but can't see her. I go outside to get some fresh air. I find myself in the alleyway next to the pub, the very place where Madeleine was throwing up last year. It's quiet and the stone walls are cool. Probably too cold in fact, especially as I've left my coat inside, but it feels like it's doing me good. Soothing me.

Listening to the creaking and clanking of the boats in the harbour, I wonder to myself if I can sneak away without anybody noticing. The quiet of my little flat is so inviting.

Valerie would no doubt make a note of it though, and I would be marked down for not having enough commitment to the paper or some such bullshit. After a few minutes I take a deep breath and go back in.

The rest of the party passes uneventfully. I decide not to say anything to Sheila or Guy for now, but to just see how things go with Valerie. I suppose it's possible I've misinterpreted her, I think optimistically, but I'm not convinced.

I spend some time chatting with our guests and towards the end of the evening I return to Jason and Simon, both of whom seem very merry.

"I hope you're not driving home," I tell them.

"Nah, Jason's girlfriend's picking him up," says Simon, and I experience a small unexpected flash of disappointment at the thought of Jason having a girlfriend, "And I shall be walking home to clear my head."

"Well that's OK then!" I say, hoping I sound light-hearted. "I don't suppose you would accompany me as far as my front door?"

"It would be an honour," says Simon, "Just tell me when."

We begin the walk home in companionable silence, although I am fairly deep in thought, about Sam and about the situation at work. Now I'm more worried because Valerie is involved. Still, at least it makes a change from thinking obsessively about Dave.

"What do you think about the farm idea, then?" Simon asks me.

"The what?" I am distracted.

"What I was saying earlier – expanding what we're doing at Ivy House Farm, working with some of Jason's kids."

I try to look as though I know what he is talking about. This must be what he was saying when I was thinking about Valerie earlier.

Simon continues, "I really like the idea. I'm wondering about whether it should be to local kids – or whether we could even offer, like, working holidays to kids from the bigger cities. Give them a chance to experience something different."

I think this is a great idea, of course. From what I saw at Ivy House Farm, it seems really effective and positive. There's something bad in me tonight though and I do something very out of character, turning Simon's enthusiastic and thoughtful conversation into an argument.

"You could do, I guess," I say, "But at the end of the day you're never going to get away from the fact you're a farmer, are you? "

I don't look at Simon as I continue, though I feel him grow quiet beside me,

"I mean... you kill animals for money. How can that be right?"

"Erm, that's not really what I'm talking about, Jamie."

"No of course not, because it would be a bit too inconvenient to talk about that side of things, wouldn't it? You can come across all caring about these kids – kids who beat up old ladies, I might add – but what about the animals you're responsible for? How about caring about them?"

What am I doing, I wonder. I think I might be losing it. Here is Russell's perfectly nice friend, talking about something really pretty great actually, and walking me home as well, yet for some reason I am being a complete bitch to him.

"I do care about them," he tells me, "Otherwise why do you think I'm walking home tonight when I could easily stay at a mate's house in town? In a few hours, while you're still tucked up in bed, I'll be out there feeding them, mucking them out, checking they're all well."

"Well yeah, of course you will, but you're not doing it for their sake, are you? It's to make sure you get a nice fat wad of cash when you kill them. Why can't you just be honest about it?"

I look at him and see he looks angry. I'm glad. I'm mean. I am on a roll and I don't know why I am picking on Simon but suddenly all of my anger at the injustice of the world has taken hold of me and I want him to feel it.

"I mean, it's bollocks isn't it, that bit about caring for the animals? If you cared, you wouldn't kill them. And all the while you expect us to feel sorry for you, poor little farmers in your massive houses, with all that land and EU subsidies. It must be really tough for you."

"You haven't got the first clue what you're on about, Jamie. I suggest we stop this conversation right now. Perhaps we'll continue it when you're sober and we can have a proper discussion."

"Bloody hell, Simon, when did you get so self-righteous?"

"Oh OK, I'm self-righteous now? I suppose you'd prefer to have that lovely bloke Dave with you, would you?"

"Don't mention him," I hiss.

"Well why not? The bloke was a prick and you know it."

"How dare you? You didn't know him."

"I heard enough from Russell. He thought he was a prick too; you didn't know that, did you? I guess you also didn't know that I had to stop him getting off with that silly tart Madeleine at last year's party?"

I stop dead.

"What?"

"You heard what I said."

Dave and Madeleine? Could this be true? Perhaps Simon's just trying to pay me back for pissing him off.

He stops too, and walks back to me. His face says it all. He's telling the truth, and regretting it.

"Forget it, Jamie, I shouldn't have said anything. We'll talk about it another time. I've got to get up in the morning and look after those animals of mine, remember? Otherwise how am I going to make my nice fat millions?"

"I'm sorry Simon, I don't know what I'm on about, I didn't mean to be rude to you. What about Dave and Madeleine? What about them?"

I begin to cry, but he is having none of it. Simon starts walking again and I have to work to keep up with him. My apology must seem pretty empty to him, I think, and we both sink into silence until we reach my house. I don't think I can take much more, and I wonder what else life is going to throw at me.

"Would you like to, do you want to, come in for a coffee?" I ask.

"No you're OK, you'd better get to bed. I'll be better off getting home."

"Please," I try again.

"No, don't worry about it."

"Right," I say, and watch him sadly as he walks off up the hill. I am standing exactly where the dead badger was, that morning all those months ago. That day marks the time that everything started to change for me, but it appears that even before that, things weren't as they seemed.

My head is full of what Simon said; what happened with Dave and Madeleine? Was it a one off? Were there others?

I am worried about Valerie and what's going to happen at work.

I am upset about Sam, and worried about my parents being upset too.

I feel like shit for being so unforgivably rude to Simon. I mean, I do quite believe what I said, but most of the people I care about are meat eaters and are part of the whole thing. He hasn't even really chosen this living for himself and even if he had, what would give me the right to talk to him like that?

Finally, and perhaps most strongly at this moment, I am really missing Mel. Lovely, stable influence on my life. I do seem to be doing a very effective job of losing everybody who is any good.

We Party in Style!

Last Friday, everybody who is anybody partied the night away at the annual *Advertiser* New Year party, held at the White Hart.

This year was a more informal event than in previous years, which have been black tie affairs. The more relaxed atmosphere was appreciated by everybody.

Relaxing

Town Mayor Neil Hughes told the *Advertiser*, "It is great to see so many of the town's business people taking a well-earned night off and relaxing together. Many thanks to the Advertiser for another enjoyable night."

Guy Wise, Editor of the Advertiser, wishes to thank everybody who attended for making the night such a success and also the owners of the White Hart – Sue and Malcolm MacDonald - and their staff.

Pictures of the night can be found on the central pages.

PART TWO

The train stopped.
The lights went out.
Soot and smoke filled the air.
A pause.
Then,
PANIC.

People were screaming, pushing, shoving; trying to break the train's windows. Gasping for air, amid the smoke and soot and the fear which was banging hard and strong against ribs and chests.

Dave stayed in his seat, he couldn't have moved if he tried. He closed his eyes. He opened them again. It was still the same.

He tried to say something but no words came out, and who would have heard him anyway?

After who knew how long, he realised the back of his head was throbbing; he must have banged it against the window when the train had stopped so suddenly.

The emergency lights in the tunnel went on and as his eyes became used to the light, Dave looked at his fellow passengers. They were dark shapes but he could make out vague features on some of them, and was that... blood? Some of them were sobbing, some of them just standing stock still and wide-eyed. Others were clasping each other and some were trying to calm everyone down; murmuring comforting, reasoning suggestions for what had just happened. It was just a power failure, an electricity surge or something.

The immediate panic died down but Dave could sense the nervous energy, the inward fight between wanting and failing to believe these innocent explanations.

Then they heard it.

The screaming.

"What's going on? What's going on?"

"I don't know."

"I'm scared."

"What the fuck's happening?"

The voices of Dave's fellow passengers were stronger now, urgent, perhaps trying to drown out the eerie sound of the people further along the train.

Dave himself still could not speak but instead watched the scene around him. All of these different people - young, old, black, white, Asian, British, foreign. From the studious ignoring of each other, customary on any standard Tube journey, these people now were looking to each other for help.

After what seemed like hours but what was in fact was only 25 minutes or so, one of the doors of the carriage was opened and Dave felt a huge relief to see police and paramedics moving into this terrifying claustrophobic space.

"Is anyone hurt?"

The passengers started shouting at once, caving in to a mass hysteria, and the emergency services staff moved through the carriage, quieting the clamour and assessing the scene. Satisfied that nobody was terribly injured, they began ushering the people out, fielding questions with vague answers and concentrating on their task of shepherding their charges to safety.

Dave walked silently in shock, with his fellow passengers. An older lady took his arm, whether to help him or help herself, he was not sure. He looked at her and felt his own blank look reflected in her eyes. They walked on.

When they reached the platform, Dave found himself surrounded once more by panic. Soot-blackened people milling about, being guided from the platform to ground-level. Some bleeding, some crying, some in hysterics. Others calm, and baffled, still trying to comprehend what had happened. Dave realised he was one of these people. He had not spoken to anyone. The old lady had let go of his arm, and been swept along by a paramedic, possibly concerned by the lady's age. Dave had continued walking though he didn't know where he was going.

He was thinking that the man on the Tube was probably right about the power surge, he was wondering if he could still get to Leicester Square and if not, how was he ever going to make his appointments today?

"Are you alright, sir?" asked a concerned-looking paramedic.

"I'm fine thanks," said Dave, and she looked as though she didn't believe him but was suddenly besieged by a man thrusting a bleeding girl aged about seven into her arms. The paramedic's attention distracted, Dave kept on walking towards the exit.

Outside it was the same; more bloody, sooty people but now mingling amongst the clean onlookers, who were trying to help, trying to find out what had happened. Looking scared, looking worried, trying to make jokes and lighten the atmosphere.

Dave avoided them, bumping his way through the crowds and trying to look as though he had just seen someone he knew ahead. That way nobody stopped him, wanted to talk to him, ask him questions. He just wanted to get away, carry on with his day as if nothing had happened. What was a power surge after all? And a load of over-reacting people? He had more important things to think about, he told himself, but he couldn't escape a feeling deep inside that something awful, something evil, had occurred. That terrifying boom must have been more than a blown circuit.

He got to the edge of the pavement and walked along the kerb a little way, hardly noticing the way that the traffic stood perfectly still. Everything seemed to be going in slow motion anyway. He sat on the kerb and caught his breath. Sirens sounded from all directions, reverberating from the buildings and ringing in his ears.

Dave was aware of the interested looks of passers-by and some of the car drivers round about. He wondered if he too was covered in dust? No way to present himself to prospective employers.

He felt an urge to check his bag. Damn, it was unzipped. He was sure he'd done that up after he bought the train ticket. He felt inside for his wallet. It was nowhere to be found. He couldn't have been... he had. He'd been bloody pick-pocketed. How the hell did that happen? His cash cards, his driving licence... all gone. As was his mobile phone. Great. Today was not going to plan.

Unzipping another compartment, he was relieved to find his building society book, and his passport, still in place. Well that was something.

Safe too were his personal documents – certificates of education, and his portfolio remained in place. He could still make his meetings. He needed to know if he looked presentable though.

"Oi, mate," he shouted to a nearby cabbie who was having a cigarette out of his window, "Have I got soot all over my face?"

"Oh yeah, just a little bit," replied the cabbie with what Dave assumed was typical cheeky cockney sarcasm, "What's happened?"

"Dunno... power surge or something."

"Oh," said the cabbie, "Do you want some of these wet wipes to clean yourself up? The missus gave 'em to me, you know, nice and refreshing in the summer."

"Um, yeah, thanks," said Dave, hoping he wasn't about to be drawn into an hour-long conversation about the cabbie's 'missus' and kids. However, he needed to clean himself up for his appointments.

Standing by the cab's open window, Dave could hear the radio reporting on the incident. They had the wrong location though, they were saying it had been at Edgware Road.

"Got that wrong," said the cabbie.

Dave thanked the man for his wet wipes and made to walk off.

"You going to be OK?" the cab driver asked.

"Yeah fine thanks, got to find a policeman – my wallet's been nicked."

There were certainly plenty of policemen about but none were very interested in Dave's missing wallet and phone, and tried gently at first, and then more impatiently, to move him along.

Great, he thought, public service at its best. It would have to wait though, if he was going to make his meeting.

He headed south, hoping that he would come across a police station on the way to Leicester Square. He had to get to these agencies though, he just had to. Otherwise he'd have nothing to use his cash cards for anyway. At least he kept his savings in the building society. The thieving bastard pickpocket was welcome to his overdraft.

The streets seemed full yet still, as Dave made his way determinedly, trying to second-guess his route. There was definitely a weird atmosphere, he was thinking, when he heard two girls sharing a cigarette outside their office talking about it.

He stopped in his tracks.

"Seven explosions," he heard, and "Al Qa'eda", although he knew that anything could be blamed on Al Qa'eda these days. Still, it grabbed his attention and he asked the girls what was happening.

"Oh haven't you heard?" one of the girls gasped.

"It's just terrible," the other one supplied, although Dave got the feeling that she was actually enjoying the drama.

"Al Qa'eda have planted seven bombs – five on trains and two on buses. Nobody's dead though, at least not yet. At least they're not saying anything yet," she corrected herself.

"Was one of these bombs... was one on a King's Cross train?"

"Yeah..." she expelled a big sigh, "Do you, like know someone who was on it?"

"Erm, maybe," said Dave, "Can I borrow your mobile please?"

"Oooh yeah, sure," said the first girl, perhaps hoping to get a story from Dave that she could gush around the office. She handed him her phone and lit another cigarette from the end of the one she was still smoking.

Both girls watched as Dave punched in Jamie's number, obviously eager for some third-party share of the exciting incident.

Nothing happened.

"Damn it," Dave said. There was no network, it seemed. The other girl offered him her phone which she assured him was on a different network and a 'really good' contract too, with loads of free texts and stuff. Despite the girl's impressive consumerism however, the bloody thing wouldn't work.

"Thanks anyway," said Dave, and left the girls to their gossiping. He spotted a phone box, with a queue of about twenty people outside it; evidently nobody's mobile was working. Dave decided to carry on his journey.

Not much later, he noticed a TV shop with a crowd of people spilling onto the pavement.

The news had reached the TV stations and it seemed like the girls had been right. Seven bombs, although there had yet to be any claim of responsibility.

Dave was beginning to realise that his mission for the day was doomed. Many people would not have been able to get to work that day, and even if they were there at the agencies he was hoping to visit, he doubted that they would want to discuss new employment opportunities. The news on the TV was beginning to draw him in anyway, in that horrible way that he'd found he couldn't stop watching footage of September 11th. He noticed he had started to shake a little, and felt cold despite the heat of the day. If he was honest, he was craving the safety he felt here, amidst this small group of strangers. All needed the same thing from each other – reassurance and reality. They could do that for each other.

Also, even through his shock, Dave couldn't help but notice there was a particularly pretty girl there who looked ashen-faced, and definitely in need of some reassurance. A small twinge nagged at him, about taking advantage of a terrible situation like this, but he pushed it away and put a friendly hand on her arm.

"Are you OK?" he asked.

Chapter Twenty

I'm going to London. To meet Guy, of all people.

It's very nearly April and the last few months at work have been painful. We've had regular meetings to discuss what's happening with regards to the merger (a summary for you: not much, or at least not much that they feel able to tell us about) and Valerie has exercised her powers to make everybody thoroughly miserable, if not paranoid, about their future prospects.

On top of this, Guy has left for good – and nobody is clear if he chose to go or was pushed, although the general consensus is that there must have been an element of coercion. He really did seem to love living and working here, but I suppose that since Valerie's come along he's not felt like top dog anymore.

Valerie's main strengths have become apparent over these last few months – she has brought with her a wealth of patronising and ill-informed opinions. She is disrespectful about pretty much everyone (including Jim and his fellow directors). She goes on and on about life in the 'real world' and has made it quite clear that our little backwater newspaper is well below her usual standards. Why doesn't she just piss off then? That's what we all want to know.

For reasons best known to herself but I think largely for her own amusement, she has been trying to get all of us at the *Advertiser* and, I'm guessing, the other papers we are set to merge with, to stab our colleagues in the back. Unfortunately for Valerie, not everybody is as completely self-interested as she so she's not getting much back – or at least not out of Sheila, Jerry or me.

We've been open with each other about the conversations she's had with us and I think she is just out to cause trouble, and inflate her own ego. Having said that, if she inflates it any more it will surely burst, splattering our office.

In between telling Jerry how he is far and away the superior journalist of the *Advertiser*, she has suggested to him that he might even have it in him to nearly meet her high standards. The honour!

Jerry laughs about it, but I can imagine he had to bite his tongue.

Valerie patronises Sheila in a very sickly sweet way, and not-very-subtly criticises Dan as a choice of husband ('He's not very career-minded is he, your Dan?', 'I suppose he's happy in his little job', 'I suppose you have to make do with what you can find in a little town'. Nice, eh?). Sometimes she tries to sound jokey but she is fooling nobody.

She has left me alone since the party, having as little to do with me as possible. I have found it impossible not to be short with her, though I try my best to be civil.

I think the worst thing is that I feel stupid for having trusted her initially. I feel like a right idiot. I know she's been derogatory about me to Jerry, hoping that he will back her up. Apparently I am not hard enough and need to toughen up. I don't follow this line of thought at all but I guess I expressed my opinions to her about the kind of things that bother me, e.g. encountering sexism at work, and I think she really believes it is everyone for themselves so I shouldn't be wasting my time thinking about these kinds of issues.

In turn, she has suggested to me that Sheila is lazy and a disruptive influence on the office and has for some reason hoped that I would support these opinions. She has been disappointed.

Anyway, the long and the short of it is that Guy has returned to London. Although he tried to support and suck up to Valerie at first – asking her opinion, praising her answers, repeating the last words of her sentences and nodding along as she pronounced one of her many opinions – I think he could see it wasn't really getting him anywhere. She would take the piss out of him to us behind his back, and be pretty rude to his face right in front of us, his staff.

In the weeks since Valerie moved in on us, Guy had become less and less his old self, which in many ways is not a bad thing but still it seemed a little sad. His complexion, to this point verging on a shade of beetroot, seemed to have paled, and his manner was actually approaching what might be described as 'subdued'. He went for lunch with Valerie one Friday and when they returned, Guy did his hand-clapping routine to bring our attention to him, and announced he would be leaving.

We all went quiet, nobody really knowing what to say. While we all find Guy annoying and a bit of a buffoon, it seemed wrong that it had come to this. It also seemed to be the start of things to come, the *Advertiser* being dismantled bit-by-bit.

With Guy's departure, Valerie has taken her management duties to a whole new level, whereby we all now feel as though we are not being trusted to behave like responsible employees. Where we have all happily managed our own workloads to this point, she now demands that we report into her our every movement. We actually have to enter details into a spreadsheet she has had her husband create, to account for every meeting, interview, phone call and article. It surely won't be long now until we have allocated toilet breaks.

Luckily for Guy, he walked straight into another job – editing a lifestyle magazine in London. I'm not quite sure how he managed it as it seems a far cry from the *Advertiser* but he says he's happy as he will be closer to his kids (from his first marriage), and was looking for a change anyway.

Which brings us back to my reason for this trip to London. At Guy's leaving drinks at the White Hart, he'd made me go to the bar with him where, warm beery breath in my face, he'd asked quietly if I would want to work for him on this new magazine. I'd stepped back a little, both from the breath and from surprise at this offer. We both knew we didn't see eye-to-eye on many things but I must admit I was quite touched he had thought of me.

Even so, my initial reaction was not one of great enthusiasm. For one thing – London? I'd left Bristol because it felt too big and busy for me. Surely to move to London would be a ridiculous thing to do?

"Think about it, Jamie," Guy had said, "You're a great writer and a hard worker, and I'd love to have you on my team."

Then he leaned across and kissed me on my cheek. You are quite rightly thinking 'urgh' but I'm too soft for my own good, and as this was the most genuine I had ever seen Guy, it got me thinking. Over the last few months, my life in Cornwall has just fallen apart really.

You don't need reminding of the series of unfortunate events of the last few months. I just thought, as I was being presented with an opportunity which might represent a new start for me, I would be foolish not to at least investigate it.

Hence my current situation; eating a cheese and mushroom pasty on the train to Paddington, idly watching the landscape blur and change on the other side of the dirty train window. I have made no promises to Guy but have said I would like to come and find out more about his offer.

Only Mum and Dad know about this and I don't think they're too happy about it. However, they understand why I need to do it. After all, in a few months' time I could easily be jobless and that is not a great situation to be in anywhere, but even less so in Cornwall.

I am well aware that this is the same journey Dave made after I'd dropped him at the station. I try not to think about it. He could have been sitting in this very seat, though. Who knows?

I know it's a useless way to think. It's been nearly ten months since I last saw him. Nearly as long as the time we spent together. How my life has changed since then. He's gone, for good, I have now accepted that. I try to put it down to one of life's weirder experiences, but it still hurts.

I am finding that far worse than the pain of having lost Dave is the fact that I have fallen out with Mel.

I still haven't spoken to her. Is that bad? I doubt myself sometimes. She's stopped trying to call me but she did send a card and present for my birthday, via Jim, who has become a regular visitor to the *Advertiser* offices. The present and card are in the same cupboard as the Christmas present she sent. Unopened.

Jim has tried to talk to me about what's happened, and gallantly taken the blame for putting Mel in a difficult situation. I don't care, it's not up to him. It was up to her whether I meant enough to be honest. Evidently not.

The rumours at work are that Jim has left his wife but whether he's moved in with Mel, I don't know. Everybody at work knows about the separation but I have not told them what I know. I may not be friends with Mel anymore but I don't want to gossip about her.

The man's obviously an idiot anyway, as he's been one of the people who employed Valerie. Is he totally stupid? To me it's become more than clear that on top of the lack of people skills, the woman is not exactly intelligent either. She just looks fairly presentable and is a good actress. She talks herself up a lot and people seem to buy it. I always think that if people need to witter on about how great they are, the chances are that they're not.

I see her and Jim talking when they're both in the office and I try to read his face. It's difficult, he plays it straight. Perhaps he does see through her, who knows? Who cares? At the end of the day he is one of the people responsible for what is happening to the *Advertiser*, and for helping create the miserable atmosphere I and my colleagues now work in. Anyway, I hope he and Mel are very happy together.

Boyfriendless and best-friendless, I find myself at Paddington station. Guy has told me to get a taxi to his office, and I am grateful I don't have to get the Tube. Ridiculous as it sounds, as millions of people use it every day, I would just rather not if I don't have to. Instead, I make my way to the rank and stand in the queue of businessmen and women, many talking loudly into their mobile phones. Suited and booted, apparently unaware of the other people around them. Wrapped up in the importance of their business here.

The heat of the city is apparent as I stand in this queue. Even at this time of year it feels slightly sticky, the air thicker than at home. The constant whirr and drone of traffic, coupled with the announcements from within the station, go some way to creating the atmosphere of urgency in the air. Is this London? I wonder. Do I want this? I think of the beaches at home, the moors. The sea.

Litter flits aimlessly in and around feet and bags here. The pavements are pocked with blackened chewing gum. Other, nameless, stains darken the paving stones. Still, there is a liveliness that I can't help but be drawn to. I shuffle along in the taxi queue, looking about me, and marvelling at the sheer number of people.

Chapter Twenty One

It takes a good 45 minutes to get to Guy's new office, even though it can't be more than four or five miles from the station. It's not much to look at – a grey 70s office block tucked away in a residential area. I don't know what I've been expecting instead. The Gherkin, maybe? St Paul's Cathedral?

Inside the office, there's even less space than we have at the *Advertiser*. Guy greets me with a big hug and loud exclamation of joy to see me – presumably at least partly for the benefit of his new team - and ushers me into the main room, where three men sit at desks facing each other, in the centre of the room. There is one empty desk which, Guy tells me, is mine if I want it.

He introduces me to the three men – Gary, Phil and Joe, and I smile and shake hands with them all then Guy makes them tell me what they do. As far as I can make out, they all seem to do a bit of everything and I get the impression that *Style & Life* magazine is not the best-organised of publications.

I glance around at the photos stuck to the walls, trying to identify the various minor celebrities pictured with my three potential new colleagues. There's even a photo of Guy grinning with his arm around a female children's TV presenter. I don't suppose the offices of *Hello!* are like this.

From what Guy's already told me about *Style & Life*, the magazine started as a weekly freebie attached to one of the London papers but just over a year ago was bought up by a wannabe media tycoon and is being transformed into a fortnightly publication priced at £1.50.

Guy takes me into his office – tinier even than his office back at the *Advertiser* - with just space enough for a tiny desk and chair. He gestures for me to take the chair and takes up his comfortable position of perching on the edge of the desk.

"So, this is it!" he tells me excitedly, "What do you think?"

"Er, well, it's difficult to say right now," I tell him, "I've only been here about three minutes."

"I know, I know, I need to show you what we're doing. I've got great plans, Jamie, great plans."

He is rubbing his hands together as he tells me this, and he does look genuinely excited. I can't help but wonder though if he's making himself be this way as a defensive reaction to Avalon getting rid of him.

"Market penetration's doubled in the last couple of months," I shudder inwardly at Guy's use of the word 'penetration' but he continues blithely, "And now I need you on board to get this place whipped into shape. The boys are great, but need a bit more drive, a bit more organisation. As you know, I'm an ideas person and I don't do detail. That's where you come in."

Ah, the old ideas vs. detail thing. Guy loves it, thinks he is a 'creative' and therefore has no need to do any actual work. No, the work side of things is left to 'details' people like me. In other words he's a lazy bastard and can't be bothered to test out his ideas to see if they actually work. Still, at least with Guy I can tell him if his ideas are crap. Then he will give me the 'don't come to me with problems, I want solutions' line.

Eventually, after enough nagging from me, if he can find a way of backing down without losing face, he will do, and will try to spin the situation to his own advantage. I really don't mind that much to be honest. As long as I am enjoying my work and my opinions are listened to, that's fine by me.

"Today I want you to spend the day with me," Guy says, "Then we can have a night out tomorrow night – you, me and the boys. During the day, perhaps you can spend some time with the lads and see what they do. It's not brain surgery, it's no different from the *Advertiser* really, except you're in a city with millions of people of different nationalities rather than a town of a hundred fishermen." Snort.

I feel slightly riled by this knock to my home town but I bite my tongue; I think it's partly my feeling guilty that I am considering leaving it behind again.

"So is it good being back near your kids?" I ask him, "When's Fiona coming to join you?"

A slightly doubtful look crosses Guy's face but he answers cheerily,

"Oh the kids are great, just great. I've been to the footie with

Kevin a couple of times, not seen much of Suzie yet but then that's eighteen-year-old girls for you. You'd know all about that, I'm sure!"

I notice he doesn't answer the question about his current wife and young family in Cornwall, and wonder if the rumours I've heard are true – that she's decided not to go to London with him. I can't say I'd blame her, I don't see Guy being great husband material. In addition to that, why would anyone uproot their kids from Cornwall to grow up in a busy, polluted city?

I smile at him and ask if I can have a drink. He directs me out of the office, along the hall to a kitchen shared with the other offices on this floor.

"Mine's a coffee," he tells me, and grins.

"That's nice," I say, and grin back.

The corridors are dark and dowdy. I pass three other doors on the way to the kitchen, each painted grey and with a blind pulled down inside the glass for privacy. There's a lady in the kitchen, around ten years older than me I'd guess, dressed in a sharp suit and stupidly high heels. She doesn't seem to fit into this dowdy building somehow. I smile and say hello but she actually doesn't even look at me, just carries on making her drinks. Nice.

When she's left the room, I look around the kitchen for cups, coffee and tea. There are a couple of cracked mugs in a cupboard and some sad-looking teabags in a Tupperware tub labelled 'Mike's'. Further investigation reveals a small jar with coffee welded to its insides. The fridge contains an open pint of milk, also labelled 'Mike's', as well as a pot of yoghurt and a sort of furry, yellow stain. I wonder if that is Mike's too. I end up going back to the magazine's office and ask what I'm meant to do.

"Oh, just take whatever's in there," Gary tells me.

"But there's nothing," I say.

"I think most people keep their stuff in their own offices," Joe says.

"Great, so have you got anything in here?"

All four men look around at each other somewhat helplessly.

"We just kind of go to Starbucks," Phil tells me.

"But that must cost loads!" I say, "Isn't there a newsagents or something nearby?"

"Oh yeah, there's a little Sainsbury's just up on the corner," says Guy.

"Right. So would you like me to go and get some stuff from there?"

"Oh would you, Jamie? That'd be great," gushes Guy and, looking at the other blokes, "I told you she'd fit in here!"

I ignore this remark for now but I am not going to be the office housewife. However, just for today I will make myself useful in this way, if only because I'm dying for a cup of tea. I get some cash from Guy then head off to Sainsbury's for some cheap mugs, teabags, coffee, milk and sugar.

When I get back, Joe takes my bags off me and he goes to make us all a drink.

"Can't have you doing everything, Jamie," he says, which makes me feel a little bit better.

While Joe's out of the room, Guy tells me a little bit more about the job he wants me to do.

"I need somebody I can rely on to keep things moving. I'm going to be busy with lots of meetings, building relationships with other publications, businesses and so on. I'll need somebody to pick up where I leave off and see things through to completion."

"So specifically what kind of things do you see me doing?" I ask, little the wiser for this explanation.

"Well, the role will evolve of course, as we go, so you could be doing anything."

"Writing? Editing? Interviews?"

"Yeah, of course, all of that..."

Guy's words trail off as his mobile phone bleeps and he checks it then starts to type out a text. This is fairly typical behaviour of Guy as well. He has the attention span of an amoeba. He chuckles to himself, which suggests he is texting somebody of the female persuasion. It never fails to amaze me how he does get quite a lot of attention. I guess not everybody sees him the way I do.

It's evident that some people are charmed by him in fact, and he's done well to get this job so quickly. I am just being a bit harsh; after all I wouldn't be here considering this job if I hated him that much. If I'm honest he makes me laugh sometimes, and I find him more exasperating than anything else.

I must admit the idea of expanding the magazine's reach and content is quite exciting and I would love to get stuck into something like this but then what about my writing? My journalism? Would that all go out of the window?

"So what do you think?" Guy asks, looking at me keenly.

"I'll have to think about it," I tell him, "I like the idea of it. I like the look of the magazine too but it seems kind of expensively produced. How's it doing financially?"

"Oh, let me worry about that side of things," says Guy vaguely and he changes the subject to the current content of the magazine and where he sees it going.

"Face it, Jamie, if you stay in Cornwall – and you know that depends on that witch Valerie and her cronies - so it is an 'if', there's nowhere to go there. Get on board with me here and the world's your lobster." Snort.

"I know what you're saying, Guy," I tell him, "Let's see how the next couple of days go, shall we?"

"Sure, sure, no hurry, no worries. We'll have a night out with the boys, see how you all get on. Bet you'll love being the only girl, eh?"

Snort.

I spend that day and the next with Guy, listening to him prattle on, then in the evening we go out for a fantastic Chinese meal in a large restaurant not far from Piccadilly Circus. The 'boys' are quite good fun actually, and I enjoy their company. I shouldn't admit this but I actually do enjoy being the only girl, and what's more I think I am picking up some interest from Joe.

He's a couple of years younger than me as I'd guessed, and is really into music and gigs, which is something I've missed about life in Bristol since being back in Cornwall. He's one of those people who seems to see a different band every week and I like the dedication he's got. I can't resist returning his smiles. What can I say? He laughs at my jokes. How could I not like him?

I drink quite a lot of red wine, and feel myself becoming more animated than I think I've been in some time. I'm telling jokes. I'm laughing a lot. Loudly. I realise I'm really excited to be here in London – it's so busy, full of so many different people.

When we leave the restaurant I wonder if that's the night over and done with, and feel a bit disappointed at the thought.

"Where to now, Guy?" asks Phil.

"Let's keep on drinking, shall we? Show Jamie a good time, eh?" Guy nudges me.

I smile and nudge him back, thinking to myself that he's OK

really. I must be drunk.

We stop at the next pub and it's absolutely packed out. No chance of a seat here. We fight our way to the bar but after ten minutes have still not been served. I can feel my face is flushed with the drink and the heat of the pub.

"Are you OK?" Guy asks me.

"Oh yeah, fine thanks, wish we could find a seat somewhere though."

"I know somewhere we could get a seat," he tells me, "And it's table service. You won't like it though."

"OK, let me guess, a strip club?" I roll my eyes.

"Let's say a gentleman's club," says Guy.

"No, let's call it what it is. A strip club," I say, "Where stupid men pay stupid girls to take their stupid clothes off. Well you lot go on if you want to, I'll get a cab back to the hotel."

"Oh don't, Jamie," says Guy, "We don't have to go there. We can just stay here and keep drinking."

"Strip club! Strip club! Strip club!" chant Phil and Gary. Joe, I notice, keeps quiet and is looking at me.

"No, you lot go," I say, after all I don't even know Phil and Gary and am not about to get into an argument with them about the sex industry, "I'm knackered anyway. I'll see you after the weekend."

I smile at them all before turning away – after all, these may be my new work colleagues and who am I to be telling them what they should and shouldn't do with their spare time? I can't deny I'm irritated though and the shine has been taken off the evening somehow. Still, the thought of my nice cool hotel room is infinitely tempting. "Jamie, hang on," Joe catches my arm as I head out of the door, "Let me walk you back to the hotel. You'll spend a fortune on a cab and it's only ten minutes' walk."

"Don't you want to go on to the club?" I ask him.

"Nah, not my thing really."

"Really?"

"Yes, really. I mean, I do like girls and everything," he looks flustered, "I'm just not really into paying them to strip for me. It's just... weird. Awkward. Definitely not a turn on."

"Well I'm glad," I tell him, and I take his arm. I know I should probably be a bit more careful – after all I'm in a city I don't really know, with a man I don't really know, but I'm still feeling the buzz of the place and it makes me a bit more carefree. And who knows when you really know somebody anyway? I thought I knew Dave and look what happened there.

On the way to the hotel, Joe talks about Guy, and asks me what I think of him. I am diplomatic. Guy is, after all, his new boss and potentially is going to be mine again as well.

"He's OK," I say, "His heart's in the right place and he will stick up for you if there's ever any problems."

"He's a bit of a twat though, isn't he?" asks Joe.

I laugh.

"I mean, he's quite old school isn't he? Quite sexist? And some of the things he comes out with..."

"I know, I know, but honestly he's not all bad."

"I'll take your word for that."

At the hotel, Joe asks if I fancy another drink, as the bar is just off the lobby and is clearly still open, still full in fact, and ringing with conversation and laughter.

I consider it for a moment. A part of me really wants to say yes but I think better of it. I don't want to sound over-confident but I can see Joe is interested in me, and although I'm enjoying his attentions, I should really be careful as we are potentially about to become work colleagues. If I'm going to take this job I've got to take it seriously.

"I'd love to," I say, "But I think I'd better just get some rest really. I'm shattered. Thanks for the offer though."

I reach up to give him a friendly hug and the next thing I know, he's heading in for a kiss, which takes me by surprise.

For the shortest moment, I close my eyes and let him kiss me. I know, what have I just said about taking this job seriously? It feels really good though. However, reality snaps me out of it, and I open my eyes to pull away. Joe looks embarrassed and I need to put this right immediately.

A cab pulls up over the road and I'm going to suggest Joe takes it but then see two other figures running to get in.

"Oh my God," I say, "Oh my God."

"What is it?" Joe is asking, looking worried, but I can't speak. My hands fly up to my face and I am dimly aware of Joe's voice in my ear, as I stare transfixed at the second figure who is just about to climb into the taxi.

This is no lookalike, no wishful thinking.

It's Dave.

Chapter Twenty Two

"Jamie, what is it?"

Mel's voice sounds slightly slurred. It's after one in the morning so I shouldn't really be phoning her but right now I can't think of anybody else I want to speak to. Perhaps she's in bed with Jim.

"Oh God, Mel, I've just... it's just..." I find I can hardly say the words.

"What, Jamie, what's wrong?"

Mel sounds genuinely worried, and it brings tears to my eyes, a lump to my throat. Makes it even harder to speak.

"Dave," I say, "I've just seen Dave."

"What?"

Any trace of sleepiness is banished from Mel's voice. I can almost feel her sit bolt upright all those miles away in Cornwall. Back home.

"What do you mean you've seen him? Where are you?"

"I'm in London," I say, realising that Jim either does not know I'm here, Valerie hasn't told him, or that he's not told Mel.

"What are you doing in London?"

"I'm visiting Guy."

"Guy who?"

"Guy Wise."

"What..?"

"Never mind that for the moment, I'll explain later. I'm too..."

I start to sob.

"Oh Jamie, Jamie, sorry for asking stupid questions. What on earth's happened? Did you say you've seen Dave? *Your* Dave?" Mel asks, incredulous.

"Yes," I gulp.

"Shit! Where did you see him? What did he say?"

"I, he, we..." I have turned into a snotty, gibbering, sobbing mess.

"Jamie, hold on," Mel tells me, "Where exactly are you? I'm coming to see you."

"You can't," I say, "It's miles, it's so late."

Inside though, I realise I want nothing more than to see Mel.

"Don't be daft," she says, "I'm coming now. I'll get Jim to drive."

Great, I think petulantly. Jim. I tell myself to snap out of it, though. This is my best friend, coming all the way to London at a moment's notice, to see me. What does it matter who drives her?

"Give me the name of your hotel. Get some sleep; I'll be with you in the morning. I'll call when we're nearly there."

"Thanks, Mel," I say quietly, and tell her how to find the hotel. I put the phone down and sit for who knows how long, staring at the TV but taking nothing in. How could I possibly take anything in right now? My tears have dried up as suddenly as they started. I feel empty. Exhausted.

My eyes feel sore and tired. Despite my emotional state, or perhaps because of it, I can feel myself dropping off to sleep. When I wake up, it's light outside and I feel a chill to my skin. I am fully clothed and my neck aches.

I get up, fill the kettle and make myself a coffee, then take a shower. The next thing I know, my mobile is buzzing away on the bedside table, threatening to jump off if I don't pick it up and answer.

"Hello?"

"Jamie, it's Mel. We're outside in the car, Jim's going to find somewhere to park. Do you want to come down and meet me?"

My eyes and brain are bleary. I splash some water on my face to try and wake myself up, then head to the lift. In the foyer I can see a car is pulled up outside, indicator light flashing. That must be them.

Mel waves at me through her car window and Jim gets out to open her door.

What a gentleman, I can't help but think, sarcastically.

My view of Mel is blocked for a moment and then I see her. Now I know why Jim's had to drive her here. Why he's got out to open her door.

Melanie, my best friend, is heavily pregnant and I had no idea.

She gives Jim a big smile as he helps her out of the car, and then stretches slightly before hobbling over to me.

For the second time in as many days, I am utterly gobsmacked.

Mel hugs me and after a moment I hug her back.

"Oh my God, Mel. What the..?"

She smiles almost shyly.

"I've wanted to tell you, Jamie, you can't imagine how much."

"I can't believe I didn't know! Oh my God, Mel," I say again, "How long..?"

"I'm about seven months now. I was pregnant when I last saw you, when we... I didn't know then, though."

I look at Jim over her shoulder and he smiles a bit uncertainly at me, like he doesn't know how I'm going to react. He seems different to his work persona; dressed in jeans and a zip-up jacket. He looks younger, more relaxed. I try a smile but am not sure how convincing it is. Really, I am more shocked than anything about Mel but I imagine he thinks I am disapproving.

"I'll go and park up somewhere," he says, "Then I'll grab a coffee and get some work done in the lobby. I'll call you in a bit."

"OK," Mel says, pulling back from me but not taking her eyes from my face, "Thanks, Jim."

"Oh my God, Mel!" I say.

She grins sheepishly. Puts her right hand on her belly self-consciously.

"Oh my God!" I say again.

"Do you want a drink of something?"

"Mm... yes please. Actually, can we get room service? I'm starving. I need some breakfast, right now!"

We go to the lift and up to my room. I can't look at her. I'm embarrassed at how I've behaved. Disgusted with myself for not being there to support her – especially given how she's come all this way when I need her, despite being heavily pregnant. She must be shattered.

She puts her arm through mine, "You're going to have to help me waddle I'm afraid."

"Shit!" I say, and I laugh. She laughs too.

"Now tell me about Dave," she commands.

"OK, let's get some room service sorted and I'll tell you all."

The shock of seeing Mel pregnant has almost taken my mind off Dave. Almost but not quite.

We get to my room, order croissants, Danish pastries, hot chocolate for Mel and a coffee for me. Then we sit next to each other on my bed, leaning against the headboard, and I tell her what happened.

When I saw Dave, he was getting into a cab. I just knew immediately it was him, even though it was dark and he was partially turned away from me.

"Dave!" I'd shouted, before I'd even had a chance to think.

He'd turned, and looked straight at me. His face, lit in the orange light of a nearby streetlamp, was a picture. Classic, jaw-dropped astonishment.

I saw him look from me to the cab, where his companion was sitting, and then back to me again.

I couldn't do anything. Just stared at him. Then he was getting into the cab and shutting the door. The car had driven off and I was left staring at the tail lights.

"Jamie? Jamie?" Joe had been saying my name, looking terribly concerned. I looked at him and saw what he essentially was – a stranger. I wondered what I was doing with him.

"It's OK," I had said, "I'm going to bed now."

Then I'd just walked off, into the hotel, leaving Joe bemused and alone on the pavement.

My head was spinning as I went to my room, and I could feel my pulse thumping against my skull. I felt sick, and light-headed, and just wanted to lie down while I could make some sense of what had just happened.

Was that Dave I'd just seen? Was it really? It couldn't have been. I must have imagined it.

He'd looked around though, when I'd shouted. He'd seen me, recognised me. I'd seen his face in the street light. It was him. It was. It could only have been him.

These thoughts went through my head again and again as I replayed the scene to myself.

I was shaking as I lay on my bed, and I wanted to pull the covers over me but I was just too tense.

What is going on? I had wondered to myself. Was I actually going mad? Had somebody spiked my drink? Was that why Joe had accompanied me back to the hotel? I really started to think that I was losing it but then the phone had rung.

"Miss Calder?" It was the hotel receptionist.

"Yes," I'd answered shakily.

"We have a call for you; the gentleman won't give his name, are you happy to take it?"

My heart started beating faster.

"OK," I'd said in a small voice. Then the next voice I had heard was his.

"Jamie?"

I'd suddenly felt really sick. I couldn't say anything.

"Jamie, are you there?"

"Oh shit," was all I could manage.

"Jamie, it's Dave."

I'd known who it was, of course I had. I just can't explain how weird it was to hear this voice I'd given up hoping I would ever hear again. The voice that had once meant so much to me. Possibly still did.

"Right," I'd said.

"I can't believe it," he had blurted out, "I couldn't believe it was you. How are you?"

"Fine," I'd answered. Pointlessly polite. Clearly untrue. How was I? What did he think? More to the point, what did he care?

"What are you doing in London?" he'd asked.

"Work."

I couldn't get more than one word out at a time.

"I shouldn't have phoned, I'm sorry."

"Well actually, you should have phoned," I'd told him, suddenly finding my voice and finding it rather cold, "But more like ten months ago."

"Yeah, right, I er, I don't know what to say. Do you want me to get lost?"

This last sentence brought about a sense of panic in me. Was I about to lose him all over again?

"No don't, please," I said quickly, mentally kicking myself for the 'please'. How desperate did that make me sound? I couldn't think of anything else to say.

"So how are you?" he asked again.

"Fine," I answered once more, "How are you?"

"I'm OK thanks. Well thanks, actually."

"Great."

"Oh God, Jamie," he burst out suddenly, "I can't believe this has happened. I can't believe it's you. Can I come and see you?"

"What, now?"

"No, no, I, erm, can't now," he said with no further explanation. My mind alighted on the image of his companion in the taxi.

"Right." I said.

"Tomorrow though?"

"OK. If you're sure you can spare the time."

"When? Where?"

"It'll have to be tomorrow evening, I'm busy during the day."

I had lined up tickets for an exhibition which I wasn't that bothered about but I wanted to make him wait – even though I wasn't sure how I would get through a whole day contemplating all of this.

"Tomorrow evening it is. Shall I come to your hotel?"

"No, don't do that. Let's meet at a pub or a bar or something."

I didn't want him at my hotel. I didn't know what would happen. How I'd be. I didn't want anybody with any kind of link to me seeing this meeting, even if it was just the barman at the hotel I was staying in.

We arranged to meet at 7.30 the following evening, and I hung up with the briefest goodbye. I was shaking, I realised, as I put the phone down, and I wanted desperately to talk to someone. Which is how I ended up phoning Mel.

"So you're going to see him?" she asks me, and I can tell she is fighting the urge to tell me what she thinks of this idea.

"Well yeah, I've got to," I say.

"You haven't *got* to do anything," she tells me firmly.

"But Mel, how can I not? I need to find out what the hell happened."

"OK, but what if he wants to get back together? What then?"

"That's not going to happen," I tell her, though I can't deny the thought has crossed my mind.

"Just say he does? What then, Jamie?"

"I, I don't know."

Mel sighs.

"Well it's just a good job we'll be staying the night," she tells me.

"You don't have to do that," I say.

"No we don't, but we're going to."

"But what about you and the baby?"

"What, do you think a night away in London is going to cause any harm?" she asks. "It is a dump, I grant you, but I think we'll get by. Anyway, I could do with a sleep now and I'd rather stay here

150

than be stuck in a car for hours again straightaway."

"How close are you to..?"

"Oh, we've still got a few weeks!" Mel laughs, "Massive though, aren't I? I don't know what's happened to me. Look at these as well."

Mel slips off her sandals and wiggles a pair of extremely swollen feet at me.

"God, Mel!" I say, "Are they OK?"

"Oh yeah, they're fine! Just a pair of huge marshmallows."

"I can't believe you've come all this way to see me," I say, stifling a sob, "When I've been such a pain in the arse as well."

"Oh shut up, you idiot. It doesn't matter. We'll talk about it all later, shall we?"

She hugs me and I squeeze her lightly, aware of the huge bump between us.

Chapter Twenty Three

On my way to the pub, I don't know what to think. How to feel.

Nervous, obviously. Scared, definitely.

Excited?

Not exactly, but I must admit I'm extremely keen for this meeting to take place, if only for the sake of finding answers to the questions which have plagued me since last July.

I see Dave as soon as I enter the pub, and he looks up from his mobile phone to me, with a look on his face that I don't think I've seen before. Unless I'm much mistaken, Dave Matthews looks scared.

He gives me a small smile and I walk over to him, hoping I look relaxed and confident yet all the while wondering how on earth I'm supposed to behave in this decidedly abnormal, in fact fairly surreal, situation.

"Hi, Jamie."

He stands to kiss me on the cheek and I let him, although I feel myself stiffen involuntarily. This physical contact does not feel natural.

"Hi," I say, and sit down at the table.

Dave sits too and pours me a glass of red wine – he's bought a bottle and has two glasses. His, I notice, is already half empty. He tops it up and then looks at me. In true soap-opera style we both then speak at once.

"How are you?" (Him).

"This is weird." (Me).

He laughs nervously, and takes a slug of his wine, his other hand nervously jiggling his phone up and down.

I determine to let him do the talking. I look at his hands. I remember them. Holding them. Feeling them on my bare skin. It makes me feel strange; the intimacy we have known now come to this utterly bewildering situation where I feel like I am actually sitting opposite a stranger, not somebody who shared my flat and my life. I wait for him to speak.

"You're right, this is weird," he pretty much babbles, "Really weird and really unexpected. I just can't help but think it's happened for a reason. I mean, it's just too much of a coincidence isn't it?"

"What, like *fate*, you mean?" I ask sarcastically. As far as I am aware, Dave doesn't think things happen for a reason – to him, they just happen.

"Well, yeah, I mean maybe," he actually looks quite embarrassed, "I mean, I don't know."

"OK, well I don't know either," I tell him, surprising myself with a surge of strength, "But there's a lot I don't know, isn't there? Like why you just disappeared with no explanation. That would be a start. What the hell happened, Dave? Where did you go? What have you been doing?"

I feel the anger making my voice wobble just a little.

"God, Jamie," Dave reaches for my hands but I move them off the table, place them in my lap, "Of course you want to know. I wish I could tell you, I wish I could explain it to myself as well as to you. The truth is, I don't really know."

I'm stunned by this pathetic answer.

"What, so you don't know what's happened in these last ten months? You don't know what you've been doing? I'll tell you what I've been doing, shall I? See if any of it jogs your memory. I dropped you at the station last July, so you could get to London for your meetings. That is, assuming you actually had any meetings. There were some bombs on the Tube; remember them? I tried to call you all day and you didn't answer your phone. Nor did you bother to call me to say you were OK. Somebody had nicked your wallet – I know that because I got called to London to see him in hospital – that's right, we thought it must be you. Dad and I travelled here overnight, terrified that you might be at death's door, only to discover it wasn't you at all. Do you want me to go on?"

I look at him, daring him to answer, knowing full well that whatever he says, it won't be right.

"Oh shit, Jamie, shit," his voice is a little quivery, "I'm so sorry. I'm so sorry I let you go through that. I did, I did try to call you..." His voice ebbs here a little, I think as he realises his answer is feeble.

"So how did that go then, Dave?" I have never known my voice so hard, my jaw so set.

"I couldn't, the... the networks were down."

"Right, and that's meant that you haven't been able to phone me in ten months, has it?" I don't let him answer, "Well that's fine. Really no problem. I mean, it was a bit embarrassing when I finally found out that you were OK but just wanted nothing to do with me. Being told that by the police was brilliant, I'm sure you can imagine. It just topped off those weeks of worrying, wondering what was going on, whether you were alive or dead. Thanks, Dave."

I am seething. Really, truly furious. Like I've never been before.

"Jamie, I'm such a twat."

"You're a bit more than that," I mutter.

"Let me explain. If I can. I'll try."

I glare at him, wordless. Daring him to explain this to me. He holds my gaze for a moment then the next thing I know, to my astonishment, his head is in his hands, he is distraught, sobbing, gasping for air, his shoulders shaking. The people at the nearby tables cast curious glances our way but soon look away when I turn my glare on them. As I look at Dave though, the man who didn't care much about anything, distraught and broken down, my anger seems to deflate.

"It was so awful," he manages to squeeze the words out, "So fucking awful."

I don't say anything but I look at his shaking hands, and this broken version of the man that I loved. I can't help but feel pity for him; an unwanted emotion that threatens to weaken my position as it erodes the hot, angry feelings from just moments before.

"I didn't know what had happened. Nobody did. Just screaming and... soot and I... I couldn't breathe. Didn't want to breathe. I think I banged my head. I... that's nothing is it?" he laughs bitterly, "Compared to those poor bastards in the next carriage."

I hold my breath. He was there then, he was on that train. I look at him. Wait for him to speak again.

"I got out of there as soon as I could," he continues, "They came for us and I just got away. Didn't try to help. Just walked."

"Well that's OK," I say quietly, thinking that in that situation nobody can know how they would react.

"It's not, is it?" Dave wipes his nose across his sleeve, and the tears return again, running down his cheeks, falling freely onto his arms, his chest, the table. He doesn't care. Not about the fact he is sitting crying his eyes out in public. Not about the people nearby, now studiously trying to ignore us. I don't suppose I would care either, if I'd been through what he has.

"Have you spoken to anybody about this?" I ask him.

"No, not really. Not at all. Not till now," his eyes meet mine. The tears seem to have stopped for the moment. I look into those familiar blue eyes, now bloodshot and shiny, and I know he is not making this up. I can see the pain there.

"I think you're in shock," I tell him, "Delayed shock. You should get some help."

"You help me, Jamie, please," he sniffles and I feel bad for thinking how pathetic he seems. I don't say anything.

"I don't know anybody else who can help."

"I don't know if I can," I tell him.

"I mean," I continue, "I don't know where you've been. What you've been doing. You told the police you wanted nothing to do with me. How do you think that made me feel, Dave? And why has it changed now? Why do you think I'd want to help you?"

"I'm sorry, I'm so sorry," the tears start again, "I didn't mean to hurt you."

"Well what were you thinking? You can't have thought it was OK to just vanish like that. You must have known I'd be worried. You could have at least just let me know you were OK."

"I wasn't thinking straight. I didn't even think about you."

That seems to have hit the nail on the head. However, I've never been through what Dave's been through. I remember what it was like, the shock of those bombs, the effect it had on the whole of Britain, across the world in fact, on people who were nowhere near the incidents themselves. If I'd been there, I think, how would I feel? I know there is such a thing as Post Traumatic Shock Disorder and I wonder if that's what Dave is experiencing.

"Well that much is obvious," I say, "So what have you been doing? Where have you been?"

I am emboldened and I want to know the answers to these questions before I can even contemplate trying to help him out.

"I miss you," he tells me, "I miss Cornwall, I want to come back."

Despite the amount of time I have spent dreaming of Dave coming back, to hear him speak those words now just doesn't feel real. I don't know how it makes me feel.

"Please Jamie, please. I hate it here. I hate London."

"You haven't answered my questions," I tell him.

He goes quiet.

"Dave," I say, "Tell me what you've been doing. Where you've been."

"In London," he sniffles.

"Doing what?"

"I've been working, doing what I was doing before. Web design."

"OK, so you were still able to work," I think to myself of how my own work helped me through the difficult time when I was most messed up about Dave. I can see how he could still have been able to work.

"What have you done with your time? Where have you lived?"

"Just in Islington," he tells me, as though it were the most natural thing in the world. I wait.

"I was living with a girl," he admits, looking down at his hands through lowered lashes. Even though I've been expecting this, I feel a bit like I've been punched in the stomach.

"Not, not like that. Well not really, not at first. It just kind of... happened."

"It just *kind of happened*?" I feel my anger resurging within me, rising like bile in my throat, "And then what happened? Where are you living now if you were living with this girl?"

"I, I'm still living there. With her."

"Oh right, oh great." I remember the figure in the taxi, "Was that her you were with last night?"

Silence.

"And does she know where you are tonight? Does she even know about me? Well, does she?"

The tears again. His tears. Sliding down his face. I am unmoved now as I contemplate all the things I didn't know, don't know, about Dave. Remembering how he came into my life so suddenly and rooted himself with me, so quickly that I never even had time to realise the things I didn't know.

"She doesn't know, does she?"

He shakes his head, looking utterly miserable.

"Poor girl," I say quietly.

"It's nothing, she's nothing serious."

"Oh well that's OK then, I just hope she knows that," I am nearly shouting, "Nothing serious like you and me, you mean? 'Cos we were so serious you just fucked off and left me without a word. Let me go mad trying to work out what happened to you. The only reason you're talking to me now is because I happened to see you on the street last night. You'd never have got in touch otherwise. What am I even doing here?"

These last words I speak to myself. I knock my drink back, knowing Dave is watching me. He has that same expression on his face. He looks scared.

"What?" I say, "Don't you like me being angry?"

"No," he responds glumly.

"Well maybe you should have thought about that before."

"Please Jamie, give me a chance to explain. The bombs, the shock, the..."

"No, Dave, forget it. I don't believe that's good enough reason for the way you've treated me. I'm sorry you were caught up in those attacks, you can believe that of me. I think you should get some help. But it's not just that, is it? You're a selfish bastard, and you don't know what you want. You certainly don't care about what I want. We haven't even started on you and Madeleine."

He looks up, "How did you..? Oh I guess Simon told you."

"Yes," I spit, "Simon did tell me. Eventually. He didn't want to."

"Oh yeah, sure he didn't."

"He didn't! He didn't say anything for ages. Why am I even bothering to argue about this with you? It was you who cheated on me. I have nothing to justify here. Nothing to argue for."

I push my chair back.

"Don't go, please," he asks so quietly I nearly miss the words.

"Oh come on," I say, "Do you really think I'm going to stick around? Why don't you go back to your girl in Islington and see if she can help you? Or, even better, you can help her and yourself by being honest with her. See if she still wants to know you. I know I don't."

With that, I turn and leave the pub. I don't look back. I can't. I hurry away, trying to put as much distance between myself and my ex-boyfriend as I can, before the inevitable happens. I find a small side street where I can stop, heaving and sobbing, nearly retching.

After all this time, I've seen him. I've got the answer I was looking for - namely that Dave is a selfish, unreliable bastard. I am better off without him but I can't feel happy about it.

A couple walk past me. The girl looks at me pityingly but her boyfriend pulls her on. I may look a little mad, I think to myself. Still, who cares? The best, and possibly worst, thing about London is the anonymity.

After ten minutes or so, I steady myself, take a deep breath and go back to the main road to hail a black cab. I want to get back to the hotel. I want to see Mel.

As I sit in the back of the cab, I look out of the window, hoping that I haven't got a chatty driver. I am deep inside my thoughts but dimly aware for the first time this year that the evenings are getting warmer and lighter. Spring is on its way.

Chapter Twenty Four

I text Mel on the way back to the hotel and when the cab pulls up outside, she is sitting in the lobby, waiting for me. She looks tired but somehow really, really well. As I walk through the door she pushes herself up from her chair and walks to meet me, concern written deep into her face.

"Are you OK?" she hugs me.

"I am, I think I am, I'm so glad you're here though."

She takes my arm and leads me through to the bar.

"How's your day been?" I ask.

"Oh it's been pretty nice actually – just lazed about, went out for lunch, had a little swim this afternoon and then dozed. Pregnancy's pretty brilliant really!"

"Where's Jim? Is he OK?"

"Oh he's fine, he's been working a lot of the day. You know what he's like."

I don't, not really. All I know of Jim is what I've seen of him in work. Of course I've jumped to my own conclusions about him being a sleazy, cheating bastard. I still can't quite shake that idea fully but I think I need to give him a chance. For Mel's sake.

"It's good of you both to come..."

"Shutuuup you idiot, you'd do the same for me."

I reflect on how very generous this is of Mel to have such faith in me, and feel tears pricking my eyes. I hope she's right.

"Yeah, well I've not been much of a friend lately have I? God Mel, I didn't even know you were pregnant."

"Oh look, we'll talk about all that some other time. Come on, let me get you a drink and you can tell me about Dave. I must admit I was relieved you weren't bringing him back here with you."

The thought of that as even a remote possibility seems ridiculous to me now but as I stand at the bar, waiting to be served, I go back over the meeting with Dave, and mull over what Mel has just said. It suggests she could have imagined me getting back together with him that easily. Am I that much of an idiot? Do other people think I am? I just feel so sad about the whole thing, and worn out. I've got the answers I've been looking for, I know Dave is safe and well and I know he would have come back with me if I'd wanted him to.

The very thing I had yearned for in the months immediately following his disappearance. Now the last thing in the world that I would want to happen.

What an anti-climax it's been.

At a small table lit by a low orange lamp, I recount everything to Mel and she listens, without interrupting.

"Oh Jamie," she says when I've finished the very sorry tale, "I'm so sorry. But bloody hell, that's just so... *weird*."

She's right – it is weird. Perhaps it's more weird than it is anything else, now I come to think of it. It's not, after all, your average tale of somebody's partner leaving them – sneaking off, getting together with somebody else. Although that did happen, it wasn't even as straightforward as that. In this day and age, with all the methods of communication available to us, I imagine most people can bring themselves to at least send a text or email. Not great but a clear signal if nothing else.

I have no doubt that the situation Dave found himself in was extremely traumatic. I got the feeling when I was with him that it may have been the first time he really comprehended what had happened on his train that day. I've heard tell of people with delayed shock and it really did seem like the first time Dave had realised his feelings.

However, before you start thinking I'm a gullible fool, I know it's not all about that. I know that doesn't go anywhere near explaining his treatment of me. It goes no way towards explaining his just disappearing as he did. His refusal to get in touch even after the police had traced him.

The intervening months have shown me how little he really had invested in our relationship. The pathetically small amount of real knowledge I had of him and his life, and the fact that he travelled with his passport and his secret savings seems to say he was ready to run at any time. In fact it is starting to seem to me that those bombs, those bloody awful attacks on London, were perhaps actually *convenient* to him. A chance, an opportunity, to run.

The thought disgusts me. Not just for me, in fact very little for me in comparison with the people who actually were killed or injured, their families and friends. Not to mention the people who live in this city who have had to get used to living with the thought at the back of their minds: it could happen again. What kind of a thoughtless, self-obsessed bastard allows something like this to be used to his advantage? I know the answer of course.

"The best thing about it," I say to Mel, "Is that now I know he's OK, I've seen for myself, and I know where he's been, I actually don't think I care about him anymore. I really don't."

Mel looks at me keenly, trying to see if I mean it and I look back at her calmly, openly. I do mean it, you see. I'm relieved, and also amazed by how somebody who once meant so much can now mean so very little. Perhaps though, it's fair to say that those feelings I had weren't actually for Dave – more for the man I thought he was.

"I believe you," says Mel, and she squeezes my arm.

We smile at each other. God, it feels good to be friends with Mel again.

"Thanks Mel," I say and watch her absent-mindedly stroking her dome-shaped tummy, "Now enough about him. And enough about me. What about you? Tell me everything. What's been going on?"

"Well," Mel leaves a dramatic pause, "I'm pregnant."

For some reason this makes me splutter my drink over the table. We both start laughing and it feels really, really good. I wipe a tear from the corner of my eye – for once a tear of laughter; it feels like the first in some time.

"I've really missed you," I tell her.

"Are you sure?"

"Of course I am, you silly cow."

"I've missed you too. You've no idea how much." Mel's eyes shine with tears.

"Hey, what's this? You're not getting emotional on me?"

"It's the pregnancy," she snivels, "Every now and then it surprises me, how emotional I feel."

"Well I'm not surprised," I say, "You're going to have a baby! It's bloody amazing!"

"Do you think so? Really? Even though it's with Jim?"

"Oh Mel, I should never have said that stuff to you. I should never have reacted like that. I don't want to make excuses but the Dave thing really messed me up. Of course I think it's amazing. And you are going to be such a brilliant mum."

I feel ashamed at how I've treated Mel, by how I was for those few months. It wasn't just Mel either – I was a bitch to poor old Simon that night, for no reason. Oh God, what an idiot. Luckily Mel at least is understanding.

"Even so, Jamie, you were right. Jim had a wife. Still has in fact... the divorce hasn't come through yet. And when I think about his kids. It's horrible. It's shit, I know it is, and I'd never normally... I mean, I don't even know my dad, I just know I hate him for walking out on me and Mum, and now here I am letting somebody leave his family for me. I just knew I couldn't let this pass me by, though. I'm sorry, I know that sounds lame. I feel awful for his family. So does he. He's not a bad person, you know."

"I know, I know, of course he's not," I say soothingly. I can't be judgmental now, there's no place for it here. I don't know Jim, his wife, or their personal circumstances. I just hope he doesn't make a habit of it, that's all. The important thing is clear now; I need to be supporting Mel and I will do that, whatever it takes.

"I know you wouldn't have done it without thinking, without being one hundred per cent sure it was the right thing to do. Of course you wouldn't."

"The *Advertiser* thing though, Jamie. I felt so shit about that. I was pissed off that Jim told me and I didn't know what to do."

I feel a bit homesick when I think of my job at the *Advertiser*. The little office not far from the sea. Eating lunch on the beach, watching the tourists enjoying themselves or flapping about, panic-stricken, fending off pasty-stealing gulls. I'm still not sure how I feel about Mel keeping quiet about the merger but I suppose I understand really, if I'm honest. She was in a difficult position. Life is complicated. It certainly seems to get harder as you get older but I think perhaps it gets better too.

"Oh look, it's water under the bridge now."

"But what are you going to do, Jamie? Does Guy want you to work here with him? Do you want to?"

"That is why I'm here, but whether I want to do it, I'm still not sure. I just don't know how much choice I've got and I don't want to end up jobless in Cornwall. I'm just going to have to do what I have to do."

"I shouldn't say this but I don't think Jim would let you lose your job."

"Well that's really nice, but what does that mean for Sheila and the others? And how would it look to them? I get to keep my job just because you and I are friends."

"No, it's not that. He really likes you, Jamie. Really. He rates you really highly and I swear that's down to your work, not because you're my friend."

"Well I guess the way I've been lately, he's got more reason to hate me than like me! I don't know though Mel, I need to think about it. I do love it at home, you know I do, but what am I going to do there? Even if I keep my job I'm scared of life going stale."

"You can help me look after the baby," Mel says, "I need you!"

"But that's the thing isn't it? You're going to have a family life soon. Things will change. They will, and that's not a bad thing, but I need to make a life of my own too. Russell's away travelling and I doubt he'll come back to Cornwall when he does return. Sheila has Dan. I don't know..."

I realise as I'm saying this that I am really envious of Mel. I suppose I'd always thought that of the two of us, it would be me who settled down first. She just didn't seem bothered by the idea.

Here we are though; me not knowing where life is going to take me – or where I'm going to be taking my life. Mel with a fully-grown-up partner, and soon to be a mother.

What happens when I want a baby? How much chance is there, really, of meeting somebody new at home? Unless I go trawling round the tourists like some people do, but I really don't fancy becoming like that. Maybe London would be a good 'last fling' for me anyway, before I find the place where I am really meant to be.

From my seat in the hotel bar I look at the street outside – still alive, still lively, though the night's long since dark and I know most places back home will be shutting up for the night. I can't deny the sheer life of this place.

"You'll be fine, Jamie," Mel assures me, "More than fine. Who knows what's around the corner? Remember how pissed off you got in Bristol and that's just a fraction of the size of London."

"But I've changed since then, Mel. And got some good work experience which should help keep me out of any more shitty jobs. Thanks to you!"

Mel shakes her head and looks a little sad.

"We'll see," I say to appease her, "Let's just see how it goes. There's no rush; Guy doesn't need to know till mid-May. Now what about your Jim? Won't he be lonely up in your room? Let's get him to come and join us, I think I ought to see if he gets the all-important

Jamie Calder seal of approval."

"It's a bit late for that," says Mel, looking at her belly.

She goes off to call their room and before long, Jim is sitting with us. He and I share a bottle of wine while Mel sips an orange juice and lemonade, eyeing our glasses enviously.

"I can't wait to have a proper drink," she says.

"Aah, poor Mel," Jim puts his arm around her and she looks at him with an expression I've never seen on Mel's face before. So this is Mel in love, I think, and I'm happy for her. I really, truly am.

As we sit and chat, I become increasingly sure that there is something very right about these two together and I can't possibly begrudge them that.

Chapter Twenty Five

On my journey to the *Style & Life* office on the Monday morning, I resolve not to mention anything about seeing Dave. Joe might think I behaved a little strangely but I have the perfect excuse for him.

"I was really, really sick. Sorry, Joe. That's why I had to rush off. Bit embarrassing really!" I smile gamely and he seems to buy it. He also looks a bit sheepish, I am guessing because of the kiss. I think we are both keen to brush the whole thing under the carpet.

"Don't worry about it," he says and turns back to his computer screen but not before giving me a reassuring smile. Everything is OK, it seems; a huge relief if I am going to stay on and work here.

"So how was the rest of the night?" I ask Gary and Phil, "And where's Guy? Not like him to be late."

They both grin at me and Gary says,

"I think he may be a bit embarrassed."

"Oh really?" It takes a lot to embarrass Guy; I wonder what could have happened.

"Well we went to Birds of Paradise," I wince at the name and roll my eyes as Gary continues, "The manager there was sucking up to Guy as he wanted a good review. He offered Guy a free private dance."

"With one of the girls, not from himself," Phil butts in.

"Yeah, anyway, Guy jumped at the chance, of course."

"Of course, who wouldn't?" I ask but my sarcasm misses its target.

"Anyway, on his way over, Guy's eyeing up the girls on the poles, having a great time, till he sees one of them's only his own fucking daughter!"

"No!" I gasp, "Suzie?!"

"Yep, I think so. Well I didn't really get her name. Guy dragged her down off the stage, screaming and shouting at her and then he got into a fight with the bouncers."

"It was pretty funny," Phil says.

"Shit! What happened then?" I ask.

"No idea. Guy got chucked out, his daughter went sobbing into the back rooms, and we stayed on and finished our drinks."

"Nice of you," I say, not sure whether I feel sorry for Guy or whether that is the ultimate in retribution. "Have you heard from him since?"

"I did text him the next day," Gary says, "He didn't reply..."

At this moment, the door swings open and in walks Guy with a black eye and a distinctly flushed face.

"Don't ask, Jamie," he says, and I don't mention that I have no need to. His loyal new workforce have wasted no time in filling me in on the details.

He keeps his eyes to the ground, ignoring the others, and heads into his office. I give him a few minutes and then knock on the door. He gestures for me to come in and leans back in his chair with his familiar hands-behind-head pose. I note his shirt armpits are slightly yellow. I guess he is doing his own washing nowadays.

"How are you getting on with the guys?"

"Oh pretty well I think, thanks Guy. They seem OK."

"They're a great bunch, aren't they?"

I don't reply that I don't think it is that great to let someone get beaten up and chucked out by bouncers and not go and see if they're OK.

"Joe's really nice," I say truthfully, and I hope diplomatically.

"Oh yeah?" Guy raises his eyebrows at me.

"Yeah," I say, "He's a nice bloke. Now I've got the whole of this week here, what do you want me to do?"

"Okay Jamie, what I really want you to do is just spend your time here usefully. I don't want you writing anything this week. I want you to watch what the others do, see how they work, and see what you think. I need ideas for improvements. I need to know if we want extra personnel. I want to know what you think of our features, advertising strategy, design, the works. I need a report writing up that I can share with the owners."

I keep listening, aware that any report I write Guy will be updated with his name before being presented to anybody.

"I'll review it and make amendments and I'll present to them. I will be paying you a consultancy fee for this you know, whether you take the job or not. We can agree a daily rate or project fee, whatever you prefer."

"Great, thanks Guy." Now this is good news; I wasn't expecting to be paid. I really wanted to come here to see if this is the next step in my life that I need to take.

"Before you begin..."

"Yes?" I ask, wondering if he is going to share with me the story of what happened with Suzie.

"Can you get me a coffee?"

I find myself really enjoying the rest of my time in London. Joe is a pleasure to work with and even Gary and Phil are good fun. They may be a bit laddish for my taste but they are actually really funny.

In the evenings I eat out at restaurants. I wander around a little aimlessly, enjoying the lighter evenings that signal the beginning of British Summer Time. I don't mind eating alone, in fact I quite enjoy it. I always have a book at the ready but if I can get away with it, I prefer to spend my time people-watching – other diners and passers-by. There is such diversity in London, it is the perfect place for just passing time without becoming bored.

I am also enjoying staying in the hotel, especially as Guy is picking up the tab.

"I'm not paying for any of your dirty movies though, Jamie!" Snort.

He takes me out for a meal on the Thursday night and asks for my opinion of his new job and the magazine in general. I think about Joe, Phil and Gary.

All three of them are great writers, and also expert in networking so that there is always a surplus of material and plenty of businesses wanting to advertise in the magazine.

There is a distinct lack of female-friendly features though; in fact the nature of the content could be expanded greatly. I suggest this to Guy,

"At the moment a lot of it is bars, pubs, clubs, restaurants, record shops... which we need to keep, but I think you're letting them manage their workload a bit too much. You need to be telling them where to go, at least some of the time. As it is, they're choosing places they think they might like and as you have just got three blokes working here, in their late 20s and early 30s, it is fairly limited. We need to expand. Where are the reviews of female clothes shops? Art galleries and museums? Beauty salons? Veggie restaurants?"

"We?" says Guy, "Does that mean you're staying?"

Did I say 'we'? I realise I did. Does that mean I feel part of this place?

"I didn't say that," I say and smile.

"I think you may have made a good move though, Guy. The *Advertiser* isn't the same anymore. It's just a bit miserable in the office most of the time, and Valerie is doing her best to cause ructions between us all."

"Silly bitch," Guy spits and I am slightly surprised to see him speak with such venom. I don't dare ask him what happened, why he left so soon, but it's pretty obvious she had a lot to do with it.

"I have to get back there, though. Busy week next week... it's the court case for those boys who mugged my neighbour. It's also," I add, hoping this may make him confess what happened last week at that seedy club, "Decision time for whether or not the strip club will be granted a licence."

He looks at me and says, "You'll be surprised to hear me say this, Jamie, but I hope not."

"Really?"

"Yes," he says, "I know I'm always joking about them but that kind of place doesn't belong in that little seaside town. And maybe I'm changing my mind about them anyway. Maybe I'm just getting old."

I don't press him on this. It must be pretty painful to think of your own daughter being paid by men to strip naked and dance for them.

I think of Suzie, who I met three years ago when she visited Guy in Cornwall. She was a quiet, shy fifteen year old then, and preferred to spend the day in her dad's office rather than venture into town or onto one of the beaches on her own. It's hard to imagine the girl she has become during the intervening years.

"Blimey, Guy, you'll be turning vegetarian next!"

"I don't think so, Jamie."

Guy takes a huge bite of his rare steak and I try to ignore the bloodiness of his meal.

Before we head off on our separate ways, Guy gives me a huge hug.

"I'm so sorry I had a go at you that night at the White Hart," he says, "You know, after Madeleine..."

I don't let him finish his sentence.

"God, Guy, I'd forgotten all about that. Don't worry at all. She is a silly little girl, and was way out of order. I had nothing to do with it though – you do know that, don't you?"

"Course I do! Think I'd be offering you the position as my right hand woman if I didn't? How about it, Jamie? Be my Deputy Editor?"

Hearing those words makes my heart lift a little. Deputy Editor! I would love to have that title. I know that *Style & Life* is just a teeny little title at the moment in the great scheme of things but we could make it bigger, and it might be just the thing I need to get moving in my career. However, I am not going to rush into a decision.

"I'll let you know, Guy," I smile, "But whatever I decide, thank you loads for thinking of me."

"You sound like I'm doing you a favour! I just want you because I think you'd do a good job."

"Well, thanks anyway."

My train journey back to Cornwall that Friday afternoon carries me out of the city and into the Home Counties, all the way through the West Country and over the River Tamar to my own home county.

The sun is shining and as the train rattles on into the evening, I watch the scenery pass by the grimy, fingerprint-smeared window. Spring is breaking through. I can feel it, almost smell it.

The journey has been a chance to reflect on the last week or so. The fact that I saw Dave again feels now more like fiction. Surely that never happened? And surely he was not such a heartless, unthinking bastard to have just skipped out of my life like that. And then expected to come back into it!

I try not to dwell on him, and think instead of Mel, Jim and the baby. Then Guy and his job offer. Gary, Phil and Joe. My new work colleagues?

Mum is waiting for me on the platform. She gives me a tight hug and ushers me back to the car.

"What's the hurry, Mum?" I ask her, laughing.

"You'll see!" she says.

I can make out a figure in the passenger seat of the car. For a moment, I think: Dave. Surely not, though? My heart lurches slightly and I feel sick. I approach the car nervously but out jumps Russell.

"What are you doing here?" I exclaim into my brother's shoulder as he encompasses me in a tight embrace.

"Get in the car, little sis," he says, "Back seat please, I'm the oldest, don't forget."

"Older," I correct him, "And anyway, Mum is the oldest."

"Thanks for the reminder," she says.

"Just shut up and get in. Back seat please, you're the youngest. He opens the back door and pushes me in, "Now shall I tell you straight away or make you guess?"

Chapter Twenty Six

Russell and I are sitting at one of the tables outside the Ship Inn. It's busy here and we are having to share our table with a nice older couple from Yorkshire, whose golden retriever keeps shuffling up to us for a fuss. We chat with the couple for a while and they say how much they love it here. Just arrived today, they are really excited to be back. Apparently they come here every year and wish they lived here. I hear this a lot and it does make me think again about whether I could really leave and live happily in London, but mostly I am dying to just talk to Russell. It has been far, far too long since we have been able to spend time together.

The tide is up in the harbour and we can hear the waves lapping high up the harbour walls. A couple of seals bob up and down near a newly arrived boat, establishing if it's a fishing boat and whether they might reasonably expect a fish or two to be thrown for them.

"I can't believe I'm going to be an aunty!" I think I may have said this about a hundred times since yesterday. Russell rolls his eyes but he looks pleased.

All the way back to Mum and Dad's from the station, Russell had kept infuriatingly quiet about why he was back home, insisting that if I couldn't guess I didn't deserve to know. When we finally got there, the reason became immediately apparent. Sitting in our front room with Dad was a clearly pregnant Cara.

I immediately understood why my brother had cut his travels short. Many questions sprang into my mind. Were Russell and Cara an 'item'? Would they be setting up home together? Was this the end of Russell's travels?

I thought it might be a bit rude to start firing these questions out so instead I just said hello to Cara and Dad, then kept quiet and looked around the room expectantly.

Everyone else looked at each other, as if unsure of who should start.

"Well, as you can see, Jamie, Cara is going to have a baby," Russell told me. "And, you guessed it, I'm going to be a dad. In about five months' time."

Before I could reply, Mum spoke up, "I'm sorry we didn't tell you before."

Dad continued, "Russell wanted to be here though, he wanted to tell you himself."

"What?" I demanded. "You already knew about this and you didn't tell me?"

Dad cast a worried look at Mum. Russell looked at me. Cara looked at her feet.

"I'm just winding you up!" I said, "Sorry. I couldn't help myself. Wow, though. I really didn't see that one coming. So what does this all mean? Are you back for good, Russ?"

"I am, at least until we might all be able to travel together. As a family."

He looked at Cara and they smiled at each other.

"You mean..."

"I mean that Cara and I are getting married. And not just because of the baby."

"Oh my God!" I couldn't help grinning at this news, and hugged them both tightly.

"Oops, sorry Cara, best not squeeze too tightly!" I looked at Mum and Dad. "So, Grandma... Grandad... excited?"

"Less of the Grandad, thanks," said Dad, "But yes – very, very excited. About the baby and about welcoming Cara into the family."

Mum disappeared and returned with a bottle of champagne and five glasses.

"We didn't think it right to celebrate without you, Jamie. Russ, you do the honours please."

We all had a drink to the baby's health and my brother's engagement. Later, Mum came to find me in the kitchen while I was washing the glasses.

"What do you think, Jamie?"

"It's brilliant isn't it!"

"Yes it is, but it must be bit difficult for you, what with the Dave thing."

I realised they had no idea I saw Dave in London. It didn't feel appropriate to mention it and take the limelight away from Russ and Cara so I kept quiet.

"Do you know what, Mum? It's not difficult. I am so pleased for Russell. I really like Cara. I'm just really, really happy for them both. The Dave thing isn't even relevant."

Cara is at home with her parents tonight and, much as I like her, it is nice to have my brother to myself just for this evening. We've got a lot of catching up to do.

"I think you'll be a great babysitter... ahem, I mean auntie," says Russell.

"Why, thank you. Though the babysitting may be difficult if I'm in London."

"Are you serious about that?"

"I don't know, I've still got to make up my mind, but what if I lose my job here? What do I do then?"

I stop myself from saying what I have been thinking all day. Despite my genuine happiness for Russell, I know that when he and Cara have the baby, life will be so different for them. Likewise with Mel. They will have to put their babies first, and their partners. I do not resent that at all but maybe it's a sign that I need to move on with my own life.

"Did you enjoy being in London though? I mean, it's pretty different from here. And don't forget, you were only there as a visitor. Could you really see yourself living there?"

"I don't know, I've got a lot of thinking to do. But listen, what I didn't say last night was that, when I was in London, I saw Dave."

"What?"

Russell looks shocked, and confused.

"Completely out of the blue. It wasn't planned or anything like that." I tell Russell the whole tale, and he looks angry.

"I knew the bloke was a tosser, but bloody hell..."

"You never told me that you didn't like him."

"Well no, I wasn't going to tell you that, was I? I just didn't take to him that well, but I went travelling a couple of weeks after we met, so I didn't really get to know him. Simon seemed pretty down on him too though."

"Simon?" I ask, "What did Simon say about Dave?"

"Oh, nothing specific, I don't think," Russell says, "I just remember some not very complimentary stuff from an email."

I think of Simon and feel bad. I can't believe how rude I was to him that night. I tell Russell about it, and also about Simon revealing what he knew about Dave and Madeleine.

"I'm not surprised he didn't tell me that," says Russell, "Although, as I was in Australia at the time, it would have been quite hard to batter Dave. That would explain why Simon was so down on him, though. I thought it was probably sour grapes."

"Enough of Dave," I say, "I have heard, and thought, that name more than enough over the last year or so."

"No problem. You know you're going to have to talk to Simon again though, don't you? In fact a bit more than that; I understand it's customary for the best man to get off with the bridesmaid..."

I look blankly at my brother until I realise what he is saying.

"Oh my God! Really, really? Yes please!" I say, and the Yorkshire couple look round at us.

"He's getting married!" I tell them, "And having a baby! And I'm going to be bridesmaid! I am going to be bridesmaid, aren't I?"

"Not if you're going to be this embarrassing... you'll make me change my mind!" Russell says, but he is grinning too.

The couple laugh, offer their congratulations, finish their drinks and get up. Their dog, who had been snoozing under the table, is immediately on his feet, shaking himself awake. I give him a pat on the head, wish them a happy holiday, then turn back to Russell.

"I would love to be your bridesmaid," I tell him, "I can't tell you how happy I am for you. I reckon you and Cara can make this restaurant idea work too. You could get Simon to supply some locally sourced products for you. And who knows, if work doesn't go well for me, you can take me on as a waitress."

"I'm sure it's not going to come to that. Although that does bring us back to your work situation; London... really? You were so happy to be back here."

"I know, I was, and I am. I'll never love anywhere as much as I love this place, but I also need to get on with my life and my career. I can't risk staying here to lose my job. Have I told you about Valerie who's been brought in to 'troubleshoot' or some such bollocks? Seems to me she's just good at causing trouble."

"Is this the woman who's time travelled from 1983?"

"The very same. She is horrible, Russell. In fact I am dreading going back to work on Monday, just because she makes it so miserable. I want to stand up to her but then I really will have scuppered all my chances."

"You've got a lot to think about, little sis."

"I have, I have, but let's not go on about that now, shall we? Let's talk about you and Cara, and little baby Jamie. Great name for a girl or a boy, you know!"

At this moment, Gail who runs the pub brings over a bottle of sparkling wine and two glasses.

"We didn't order that," I say, "Think it must be someone else's?"

"No, no," she says, "There was a couple sitting at this table who asked for this to be brought to you with their congratulations. They said they'd really enjoyed talking to you."

"Wow," Russell and I say together, then look at each other and laugh. I am so touched by the kindness of these strangers, and as Gail pops the cork from the bottle, I look at my brother sitting opposite me, and feel happier than I have for a very long time.

Russell walks me home before returning to Mum and Dad's. I am giddy from the drink and from seeing my brother again. Could I really leave here just when he's got back? I don't know. Probably best not to think about it now.

He wants to come in and carry on drinking.

"I don't think so," I say, "I'm shattered, and anyway, we might disturb Mrs Butters. She's not been sleeping well since she was attacked."

"Poor woman, it must have been really scary for her."

"I know. It's the court case this week, maybe that will help her get over it a bit better."

"Oh yeah, Simon said something about that. I hope that justice is served."

"Me too, me too. Thanks for a great evening, Russ. It's so good to see you again."

"You too. Onwards and upwards, eh, little sis?"

Russell gives me a great big squeeze of a hug, and is on his way. I close the door and think about what he said about Simon and sour grapes. It sounds like he was interested in Madeleine; no wonder he was pissed off about Dave and her kissing.

I check my reaction to the thought of what happened between Dave and Madeleine but there seems to be nothing. I think it has taken me seeing Dave again to realise that actually there is really nothing there anymore.

The thought makes me smile and I sit up for a while on my own, listening to music and relaxing in my lovely flat; truly my own space once again.

Chapter Twenty Seven

On Monday morning, I am relieved to find that Valerie is not around.

"Did you enjoy your time off, Jamie?" Jerry asks me.

Nobody but Sheila, Valerie and Jim should be aware that I have been in London with Guy, but I look at Jerry to see if this is a loaded question. Valerie is so indiscreet that I wouldn't put it past her.

I still can't believe that I liked Valerie to begin with. What an idiot I must be! Trusting Dave, trusting Valerie. I am not going to be anywhere near so gullible in the future.

"Yes thanks, Jerry; anything much happen here?"

"Well, they've appointed this bloke Marcus from Torbay as temporary Editor till everything is sorted with the merger. He'll be here three days a week, seems like an OK bloke. Also, great news; Valerie's not back till Wednesday."

I smile at this but don't say anything about Valerie. Best to just be diplomatic in the office, and not say anything either way. I'm pleased we've got another Editor though, as Valerie fulfilling that role really was not working well. For one thing, despite her claims of multi-skilled perfection, it turns out she's actually not very good at editing. Or writing. Or managing people.

The front door opens and Jim comes in, followed closely by a man in a short-sleeved shirt, tank top and glasses. Jim smiles at me, and comes over to my desk.

"Jamie, this is Marcus," he says, and explains Marcus' role to me. There is no indication that Jim knows me in anything more than a work capacity, and I find it hard to pair Professional Jim with the Jim I met in London with Mel.

"Do you fancy a coffee and a chat, Jamie?" Marcus asks, "Just so we can get to know each other a bit?"

"That would be great," I smile.

"Let me get them," Marcus says, "And maybe you can get me

some of your articles to have a look through."

I'm already impressed. *He* is making me a coffee! Still, I must remember my new rule about not trusting so easily.

"I'll leave you two to it then," Jim says and heads into what was previously Guy's office.

I am at my computer, pulling up old files for Marcus to look through. I pick a selection but make sure I've got a number of those I've written about the gang, as those are the ones I am most proud of.

I notice a sudden hush in the office at the sound of the door opening and as I look up, my heart sinks when I see Valerie breeze in. I look at Jerry, who shrugs at me.

"Good morning, everybody!"

She is in one of her disingenuously friendly moods but is greeted only by a few grudgingly muttered hellos. She doesn't seem to notice but goes straight into the office where Jim is.

"Ah, Valerie," I hear him say.

"You rang?" she says, giving one of her giggles which I suppose she believes are girlish.

Jim smiles tightly, ushers her in and shuts the door behind them.

I notice the blinds are down, which is unusual. Guy used to have them open so he could keep an eye on us all. Snort.

Marcus appears with our drinks and pulls up a chair. I am explaining to him about the gang storyline and how it is the trial later on in the day but the voices in the office become increasingly hard to ignore. Valerie is practically shrieking. She flings the door open.

"You'll regret this! Don't forget who I know in this business."

"OK Valerie, sure." Jim is clearly trying to keep cool but sounds fairly annoyed. "Do what you will. Go running to Piers or whoever."

"Oh I will, don't you worry."

With that, the office door is flung open and Valerie, red of face and wild of hair, comes flouncing out. She glares at me, or perhaps at Marcus, I'm not sure, pushes her way through to the door and then is gone, letting a blast of fresh sea air in on her way.

"Ding dong, the witch is dead," I hear Jerry sing quietly.

I look at Marcus and am pretty sure he is holding back a smile but he just nods his head attentively, as if nothing has happened, and asks if he can come with me to the magistrates' court this afternoon.

The atmosphere in the office starts to feel like that at school on the last day of term. People are smiling, joking, and laughing. It's only now that I fully realise just how bad it had got during Valerie's reign. The day improves further with the diplomatic confirmation from Jim that she is gone for good.

"Now, you probably all heard Valerie's... outburst... just then," he says. "I'm afraid she was just a bit upset because we don't require her services any longer. You guys have got Marcus now, and I'm pleased to say we should be able to make an announcement in the next week or so about the restructure."

We all look at each other, knowing that this is the end of the *Advertiser*. I think we are all relieved that we are going to find out at last what the future holds, but at the same time a little scared. At least I have another job offer; I'm very lucky, I know.

"Thanks for your patience throughout; it has been really appreciated, I can assure you. Now please carry on as normal and make this the best edition of the *Advertiser* yet..."

Jim's mobile begins to ring in his pocket. He looks irritated but checks the screen.

"Excuse me a minute," he says, and goes into the private office. Seconds later he rushes out, car keys in hand.

"I'm so sorry, but I've got to go, right now. I will be back as soon as I can. Sorry, sorry."

He looks flustered and my thoughts are immediately of Mel. Everybody else looks slightly nonplussed so I adopt the same expression. My phone vibrates on my desk. A text message.

"Jamie this is it! It's a bit early but the baby's on its way. Send me some good vibes, I'll let you know news asap. Xxx P.S. Ow."

This is turning into a very eventful day.

Marcus and I buy sandwiches and he drives me to the magistrates' court.

There are a few people outside the courtroom. As it is a Youth Court case, entrance is restricted. I recognise a couple of people from the local radio station and a teacher from the secondary school. I see Simon and Jason, standing together. Jason sees me, waves, and nudges Simon, who looks up and gives me a small smile.

I haven't seen Simon to speak to since my outburst and I determine to find a moment to speak to him today, if I can get away from Marcus for a few minutes. I wonder if he's here as something to do with his farm project.

There are a few other people I recognise from town. I guess what has happened, not just to Mrs Butters but to town life in general, has affected everyone.

I see Caroline nearby and say hello.

"Mum couldn't come," she says, "Well she could but she's so tired and I don't see what good it would do. I can tell her what happens. She doesn't need to see them and be reminded of it all over again."

I smile and introduce her to Marcus.

"So you're Jamie's new boss?" Caroline says.

"Yes, sort of..." Marcus begins but she cuts him off.

"Well she deserves a promotion. Have you seen what she's been doing with this story? The *Advertiser* has taken on a new tone since she joined it. I couldn't really read it before to be honest but I like it now. It's not just your usual local rag."

I blush. Marcus just smiles and says it's good to hear that people like their local paper.

Shortly afterwards, a teenage boy walks out, accompanied by a relieved-looking woman who I assume is his mother. Dressed in a suit, he does not look scary. He looks very young, like he is playing at dressing up.

There is no sign of the second boy, which I assume means he is being taken into custody. This is further confirmed by a very tearful woman exiting the court, supported by a man in a suit. She looks at us all, standing around to find out her son's fate, sobs, and runs out of the building.

Shortly afterwards, we are able to get the details from one of the court officials.

The boy who I think actually confessed to everything, and who we saw leaving the court, has been given a non-custodial sentence and community service order. I wonder if he might end up with Jason.

Matthew Browning, who carried out the actual attack, has, as I guessed, been given a custodial sentence.

Caroline looks at me, "I'd better go and give Mum the news."

"Okay," I say, putting my hand on her arm, "Hopefully this will draw a line under it for you all now."

I look for both Jason and Simon but only Jason is still there. I take Marcus over and introduce them to each other.

"Ah, I've read about you, sir," Marcus says in his broad Devonian drawl.

"Have you, now?" says Jason, "All courtesy of our Jamie, eh? She's been doing a grand job you know."

"So I've been told," says Marcus and smiles at me. I blush for the second time this afternoon.

Jason fills us in on some of the details of the case. He knows Matthew Browning, the boy who'd carried out the attack, as he had been responsible for a community service order the boy was fulfilling the previous year.

The boy's father has apparently been in and out of prison for years, and sadly it looks like his son is following suit.

"What about the other lad?" I ask.

"Yeah, I don't know. I've certainly not met him before. Think this might have been enough for him, seeing that old lady kicked about. Hopefully he'll get through his service and move on to something a bit more useful than vandalism and mugging people."

"Will he come to you?" I ask.

"I don't know; we'll have to see. I think I've finally got Simon's project authorised though. Oakdale's going to become another approved project for rehabilitating kids who've got into trouble."

"That's brilliant," I say, and wish Simon was there so I could congratulate him. I hope he hasn't left early to get away from me but I take comfort from the fact that he did at least smile when he saw me.

As we drive back to town, the sun escapes its cloud cover just as we tip over the top of the hill, and we see it spill its glorious rays across the sea. My heart leaps for joy.

I check my phone to see if there is any news from Mel. An envelope icon tells me there's a text message waiting but it's just from Sheila.

"Great news, Jamie, strip club's not happening. Thought you'd like to know. Sx"

I laugh out loud.

"What's so funny?" Marcus asks, glancing at me and smiling.

"Oh nothing, I'm just happy," I say. "Valerie's gone, that lad's been locked up, and now the strip club's been refused permission to open."

"A strip club?" Marcus exclaims, "Here? No way, not in a

million years."

"That's exactly what I said."

My phone starts vibrating in my hand. It's Jim's number. This could be awkward.

"Hello?" I say, "Is everything OK?"

"Jamie, it's Jim, can you get to the hospital? I need to get back to the office, just for an hour. Can you come and sit with Mel? She's asked for you particularly. They reckon she's still a few hours off having the baby."

"Yep, erm, OK, I'll see what I can do."

"Is Marcus around? You can tell him. He knows what's going on."

"OK, sure, that makes things a bit easier. I'm in the car with him now."

I quickly fill Marcus in on the situation.

"Blimey, it's all go round here. Is it always like this?"

"No, no," I grin, "Normally it's fairly calm. Verging on boring for some."

"I'll take your word for that. Now tell me which way to go. I can drop you at the hospital and bring Jim back to the office."

Chapter Twenty Eight

At the hospital I give Mel's name and am directed to the midwife-led unit where I am greeted by a friendly orderly. She shows me to Mel's room. I knock on the door and Jim answers.

Inside, Mel, dressed in an over-sized white t-shirt, is sitting on an exercise ball, bouncing gently up and down. In her hand is a mouthpiece attached to a tube.

Jim speaks first, "Thanks for coming, Jamie, I'm sorry to do this to you. Yes, Mel, and you. I know, I know."

Mel is jokingly glaring at Jim.

"I shouldn't go, I know I shouldn't, but Mel's insisted she'll be OK if you're here."

"I'll be back as soon as I can," Jim lifts Mel's chin and kisses her firmly on the forehead. "Now don't you go having that baby while I'm gone!"

"Oh my God, Mel, oh my God!" I say, when Jim is out of the room. "You're going to have a baby."

Mel rolls her eyes and at the same time pushes the mouthpiece between her lips, inhaling deeply.

When she is finished, she speaks. "You don't say! God I knew it was going to be painful but hadn't quite reckoned on this! And the midwife says it's not even full-blown labour yet!"

I don't know what to do. I realise what it must be like for men in this situation. Especially when the midwife comes in and shuffles Mel onto the bed. She attaches Mel to a machine and suddenly I can hear it. The baby's heartbeat.

My tears take me by surprise. What a sound. *Whoosh, whoosh, whoosh.* It is so fast, and so other-worldly. This is the sound of life and it seems to me that it beats scan pictures hands-down.

Mel is looking intently at the midwife.

"Everything sounds fine, dear. Let's just keep you here for a while to get a good ten minutes though, shall we? Can you manage that?"

"Of course," Mel says. "Oh, sorry, this is my friend Jamie. Jim's had to go out. Don't look at me like that! I said he could, it's just for a while and I'm not on my own. Come sit over here, Jamie."

So I sit next to Mel and I watch the numbers on the machine. Mel explains one is for the baby's heartbeat, which is currently 148.

"Isn't that really fast?" I ask, realising I know absolutely nothing about this. I can barely imagine what Mel is feeling – physically or emotionally.

"It's fine," Mel says, and shows me on the printout where the heartbeat is shown. It goes up and down a bit, which she says is what is meant to happen. The lines which she says indicate her contractions seem to be getting higher on the chart, and closer together. She says that's fine too.

I am in awe and finding it hard to think of anything to say. This is the most intense experience ever and I am honoured to be here with my friend.

To try and take Mel's mind off the pain, I tell her about the boys' sentencing. And the strip club. Then I think of Valerie.

"Ah yes, I can finally say that Jim absolutely hates that woman! Oh, here we go again." Mel is sucking on the mouthpiece once more. I put my hand on her arm and leave it there. I look at the machine. The baby's heart rate has slowed to 126. I think of it inside Mel, having no idea of what is about to happen to it. It will soon be out here, in the world. Beginning its life, with all its inevitable highs and lows, excitement and disappointment. I wonder what life will hold for it.

The midwife comes in shortly after and checks the printout.

"I think we'll just keep this on for a little while longer," she says. Mel looks up sharply.

"I don't think it's anything to worry about," the midwife says, "Your contractions are just coming a bit quicker than I'd expected. And the baby's heart rate is slowing a bit but it seems to be mirroring the contractions, which is absolutely fine."

I look at Mel, and I look at the midwife. I feel more of a spare part than ever but I don't care. I can see Mel is scared now and I just wish I could do something for her.

"Oh my God, Jamie, I just want this to be over with now," she says, "And I'm glad you're here but I want Jim too."

"Of course you do, Mel. Of course you do. He'll be back soon." I look at the clock. "Look, I've been here thirty five minutes, Jim said he'll only be an hour so it's not long now."

Mel is suddenly back on the gas and air again. Her face looks red, and her eyes are closed.

"Breathe through it, Mel," the midwife speaks firmly. "Just breathe through it."

Mel's eyes remain screwed shut whilst she takes a deep inhalation on the tube. Her knuckles are white, hand clamped onto the handle. I don't rate anyone's chances in trying to wrestle that away from her.

"It's coming, isn't it?" she asks the midwife, when she's finally through the worst of the pain.

"Erm, let's see, shall we? I think it's time for another examination. Do you want Jamie to leave the room while I examine you?"

"No! Don't go, Jamie. You don't mind staying, do you?"

"No, Mel, of course not."

I smile at my friend, even though I feel like crying. She looks so young suddenly, with no make-up and her sweat-dampened hair tucked behind her ears.

The midwife lays a sheet over Mel's lower half and sits on the edge of the bed. She reaches down and looks at Mel while she's doing so. She smiles.

"Well, Mel, you're full of surprises, aren't you? You're nearly there. That's happened fast."

Mel doesn't answer as she is once again on the gas and air.

"Okay, now I've got to leave my hand where it is while you're contracting," the midwife tells her, "I'm sorry, Mel, but just concentrate on what you're doing. Breathe in, breathe in, that's right."

I don't know where to look. I am also starting to panic slightly. Where is Jim? Where the hell is he? This is his baby, he should be here for this.

When Mel's through the contraction I offer to call Jim.

"Yes, please Jamie, tell him to get here, now!"

I ring Jim's phone and he answers.

"Oh my God, sorry Jamie, I'm still at the office. Is Mel OK?"

"Yes she's OK, but why are you still there? She's about to have the baby, for Christ's sake!" I almost shout at him, his position of authority forgotten for now.

"What? But when I left they said it would still be a few hours!"

"Yes well apparently Mel's body says otherwise. Shit, Jim, you've got to get here."

"I will, tell her I'm on my way." I hear Jim calling Marcus' name, as he hastily ends the phone call.

I re-enter the room.

"He's on his way," I smile at Mel but she has no time to answer as she is once again sucking intently on the mouthpiece in her hand.

I stand by the bed, watching Mel, watching the midwife, wondering what on earth I can possibly do to help. Nothing. It is clear there is nothing I can do. My friend has gone into herself, she is listening to the midwife's instructions and closing her eyes against the pain.

"I think you're ready to push," the midwife tells Mel and I see my friend's eyes open in panic as she looks for Jim.

"He'll be here any minute," I tell her, and hope to God that it's true.

"Are you ready, Mel? Now push!" The midwife tells her.

Mel grits her teeth and her face grows redder.

"Focus all your energy into pushing," says the midwife, "The less shouting and screaming, the more energy you have for your baby."

Well I've never heard Mel shout or scream, and my friend somehow, amazingly, retains her dignity even through this excruciating situation.

"You're doing great," says the midwife, when the pushing is over, "Just great. Now rest for a moment until I tell you to push again."

At that moment, the door opens and Jim rushes in. Even through her pain, Mel's face lights up at the sight of him.

"Oh my God Mel, I'm so..."

Mel holds her hand up, and the midwife asks if she is feeling the urge to push. Mel nods.

"Shall I go?" I whisper to Jim but Mel hears me. She shakes her head.

"No!" she shouts, as pain grips her once more. My eyes fill with tears as I watch her, and I glance at Jim to see him gazing, rapt, at his girlfriend.

The midwife is looking intently between Mel's legs.

"Well, this one's not hanging about," she says, "I can see its hair already!"

She gently takes Mel's hand and guides it to where the top of her baby's head is. Mel gasps.

"That's what we're here for," says the midwife, "Now you know it's there, it's just waiting to say hello to its Mummy and Daddy. It wants to be out now so next time I say push, I want you to push for all you're worth!"

Jim is at Mel's side and I stand back a little. It's lovely that she wants me here but this is their moment. Their baby. Mel is pushing again and the midwife talks encouragingly to her.

"Next time, Mel, I think it's going to be the next push!"

She's right. Even she seems surprised by the speed, but on the next push, there is a slippery sound, and a huge gasp from Mel and then a cry. A baby's cry. I can't hold back my tears. I have never, ever, witnessed anything so truly magical.

The midwife is holding a bloodied, wailing bundle of life and she lays it on Mel's chest.

"Mel, Jim, you have a little girl," she says and Mel bursts into tears. I can see Jim's shoulders shaking. I sit down quietly, not wanting to intrude and actually glad to rest my wobbly legs. From here, I watch the rest of the scene unfold before me, as Jim and Mel meet their daughter for the first time.

Chapter Twenty Nine

It's the middle of May and the first really warm day of the year. Whilst the sea carries a soft breeze to shore, I can still feel the heat of the sun on my face. I walk down to town, mixing with the tourists who wander slowly and happily hand-in-hand or, slightly less relaxed, pulled along by their excited dogs.

From behind my sunglasses, I look at people's faces as they slowly learn to relax, away from the day-to-day chores of home and relieved to have the weight of stressful or tedious jobs lifted from them, if only for a week or two. At the harbour I turn left, towards the surfing beach, and make my way along the rocky cliff path until I am way up high where the gulls glide lazily on the currents of air. I can look back down at the town and its busy streets, then along to the stretch of beach where children play and dogs bark at the waves.

Sam used to love the beach. He would never tire of it. I remember the way he would run across the sand, his tail aloft as he smelled the air. He'd find a stick or a forgotten ball and bring it to me, dropping it a few metres away and barking at me to throw it for him. Into the sea he would go, jumping in high arcs through the shallows and then swimming with his nose held clear of the water, white paws just visible, paddling quickly to retrieve the object and then bring it back to me. Again he would drop it. Again he would bark. Sometimes he'd let me throw it for him again, sometimes he'd dash to it just as I was bending down and run off so I would chase him. He was a happy dog, a healthy dog, and he lived his full life. I'm happy for him but I miss him.

There are maybe 20 surfers in the sea, sealed into their full-length wetsuits. I imagine how they are feeling, alive in the cold, fresh water, faces burning from the salt, wind and sun. Exhilarated. Free.

A slightly overweight but happy-looking couple come puffing up the path towards me, faces red in the sun. They say hello and stop nearby, hands on hips, soaking up the view and catching their breath.

I walk on past them, down to the beach. At the bottom of the steps I stop to take off my trainers and socks, rolling up my jeans and sinking my feet into the cool damp sand.

Putting my headphones in my ears, I switch on my MP3 player at full volume and set it to 'shuffle'. I let the music wash over me like the waves over the beach, and I walk firmly, pressing each footprint purposefully into the tiny, damp granules of sand. From up high the beach looked almost white but now I'm here, up close, it is a warm yellow, gently golden, slowly warming in the generous sunshine.

Halfway along the beach I sit down, pulling off my jumper and making it into a pillow. I put my cap back on and tuck my hair up inside it, push my bag beneath my legs and recline, watching other people walk by. I had only meant to stop for a short while but the sunshine and the music make me relax. There's no rush for anything today and I think it will do me good to linger here a while. Track after track plays, each one seeming to have been selected perfectly for this time and place, as though the MP3 player has the ability to choose for particular moments in time.

I watch a man with his two young boys, trying to skim stones across the water but with little success. They laugh with each other and he lines up the two boys to take a photo. It brings tears to my eyes and I don't know quite why. I let the salt water trickle down my cheeks, feeling that nobody will notice me in my sunglasses and cap.

As the trio wander off again along the shoreline, the smaller of the two boys picks up a large stick to throw at the water, but his unpractised arm means he nearly hits his Dad in the face instead. It makes me smile and the man looks up, sees my amusement, and grins.

Something about this simple, straightforward momentary contact with a stranger now lifts my mood and I'm glad, although I didn't mind the tears really. They're OK too. I need to feel sad sometimes, and to know that I'm sad. It's a good thing.

A little further along the beach sit an older, white-haired couple in deckchairs, sheltered from the breeze by one of the small outcrops of rock. They both have their trousers rolled up above their knees and sit next to each other, facing opposite ways. They look happy, I think, together, and I imagine they have been married for a good long time. I am pleased for them, if a little envious, and a small hope enters me that maybe this could still happen for me. It's been a long time since I hoped that Dave would be this person for me, and my reactive resolve of 'never again' has started to mellow just a little. I know it's a long way off yet though.

I think of calling Mel, but I decide to leave it; it's only about 10am and I know she tries to have a nap with the baby at this time of day. She's not getting much sleep during the night, from what she tells me. Jim can't do much as she's still breastfeeding so she lets him turn over and go back to sleep while she holds Lucy to her and gazes into those big blue eyes which watch her unwaveringly as she feeds.

There's a lot of chattering and laughter behind me. I turn to see a group of boys in school uniform, heading down the steps clutching clipboards and sketchpads. They head unthinkingly towards the couple in deckchairs, as if they haven't even noticed their presence, and perch themselves on the rocks right next to them, looking back at the town. The couple look at each other, smile, and get up, moving their chairs away. Not through meanness to the boys, I think; there's no bad feeling in these actions. Understandably, the couple just want to hang on to their peace and quiet. I don't blame them.

It's funny watching the different people down here. The surfers, the joggers, the schoolboys, the couples. There are people in shorts and t-shirts and yet others in waterproofs and walking gear; a clash of seasons as spring and summer run headlong into each other.

Further down the beach, I see a glamorous-looking woman in jeans and knee-length boots which I can only guess are expensive, posing in front of a camera held by a tall, flash-looking man in a brown suede jacket and with a mane of shiny grey hair. The woman tosses her own, glossy black, hair away from her face and pushes her shoulders back, holding this practised pose for what seems like ages. There are two girls with this pair, the older one in a grey dress, black tights and boots. The other girl looks out of place with the others, dressed as she is in jeans, a stripy jumper and wellies, though in my opinion she's the only one dressed for the beach. I'm guessing they're staying either at a swanky hotel or have arrived in town on one of the large expensive boats which have turned up in the harbour over the last few days. I look down at the chipped nail varnish on my toes, my scruffy jeans and faded top, all scattered with sand, and feel happy with who I am.

I close my eyes behind my glasses and listen to the waves crashing against the Belle and Sebastian song that's now playing –

A Summer Wasting. The idea sounds very appealing to me, as although last summer was a summer wasted, it was not in a good way. This year I would like to just hang out at home, loaf around on the beaches, and try and pick up my surfing once more. I have had my fill of seriousness, and drama, and I'm determined that these next few months are going to be different. To think I could have been in London now. I'm so glad I'm not. I wonder how Guy is getting on and whether he and Suzie are back on speaking terms. Poor old Guy, but still I can't help but hope it's a lesson well-learned for him.

Slowly, slowly, without even realising, I drift off, and doze lightly, vaguely aware from time-to-time of where I am and that my mouth is gaping slightly open. I'm possibly even dribbling a little but who cares? My mind plays with its dreams which come and go with my consciousness; none of them vivid enough to hold onto or understand from one moment to the next.

Then all of a sudden, a cold wet nose is thrust into my face and I sit bolt upright, finding myself face-to-face with a skinny border collie. I laugh and she licks my ear, refusing to sit still as I try to get her to sit. As I look around for her owner, I am accosted by another, larger, collie, who jumps playfully at my shoulders and inadvertently clips the other dog around the ear. I ruffle their fur and they jostle each other for my attention and then both tumble to the sand, rolling onto their backs.

"Ruby! Bella!" I hear a man's voice a few metres away, and turn as he shouts an apology to me.

"It's OK!" I respond. I know these two dogs and I know who their owner is, without even looking. I turn to see Simon. The two dogs run up to him then back towards me, over-excited and unsure of what to do next. I call them over, hoping Simon doesn't mind, and I continue to fuss them as he approaches. I'm not sure yet if he's recognised me so I take my cap off and see recognition register on his face.

"Jamie! I thought you were some sun-starved tourist!"

"I'm afraid not," I say, "How are you?"

I've not forgotten our last meeting. I'd been meaning to apologise but somehow I still haven't found the time. Well let's be honest, I've avoided it. I feel embarrassed and ashamed.

"I'm fine thanks, how are you getting on?" he looks at his two dogs who are continuing to clamber over me and one another, "Sorry about these two by the way."

"Oh don't be daft, you know I love dogs!"

"Yeah, I was sorry to hear about Sam, by the way. Russell told me. He was a lovely dog."

"He was," I say, "And these two are as well! Come here, you idiots... I remember when Sam was like this. It doesn't feel like they ever calm down, does it? What brings you down to the beach then?"

"Oh it's these two, they've been pestering me to come down here. They say they're bored of sheep, and they wouldn't shut up about it so I had to give in."

The two collies, realising he is talking about them, move to their owner's side, looking up at him adoringly and wagging their tails, knocking sand about.

"I thought a bit of sea air would be good for me too," Simon continues, "Just getting over a bit of a cold."

As if to prove it, he brings a large hanky out of the pocket of his fleece and blows his nose.

"Well this sunshine should sort you out too," I say, inwardly kicking myself for talking about the weather, trying to avoid any awkwardness through the mundane small talk. I am trying to build up my nerve to apologise but I am reluctant to acknowledge my own stupidity and rudeness.

"I don't suppose you fancy a coffee?" Simon asks me.

"A cup of tea would be lovely," I say.

"Did I ask if you wanted a cup of tea?" He grins at me, "Oh OK then, come on."

I let him pull me to my feet and, grabbing my trainers, bag and jumper, I join him and the two dogs as they walk along to the kiosk. Simon insists on paying and buys a bag of chips too, which he suggests we eat at the harbour. He tucks them under his arm and the aroma of hot chips soaked in vinegar seeps into the air, making me hungry. We walk along companionably, occasionally shouting to Ruby and Bella, who chase each other up and down towards the shoreline and, all confident and full of themselves on their day off at the beach, barking at other dogs in an amiable manner.

"Simon," I say, knowing I have to, "I'm really sorry I behaved like such a twat. I had no right to do that, and I know I was totally out of order."

"Oh don't worry about it," he doesn't look at me.

"No, I should worry about it," I say, "It was really rude, to say the least, and completely uncalled for."

"Well I was quite rude to you as well."

"Yes but you were right. And I wanted to say that actually I think what you are doing at the farm is brilliant. I was kind of hoping we might be able to do something about it in the paper, actually. Only I thought you might tell me to piss off."

"As if I'd do that," he turns and smiles at me, "Would you really want to put it in the paper though? That'd be brilliant!"

"Bloody hell Simon, of course I would!"

"So... let me make sure I've got this straight," he says, "You don't hate me for being a murdering farmer?"

"I don't, I can't. I've been a judgmental cow this last year. Maybe all my life actually..."

He tells me that the first lot of kids are coming to stay in just a few weeks' time and sounds really excited about it.

"Well I hope that it goes really well, for you and for them. Did you know I was in trouble when I was a teenager? Nothing major," I add quickly.

"Ah yes, Russell did mention something but was a bit vague about it. What exactly did you do?"

Inwardly, I make a note to kick my brother when I see him next.

"I guess I was a bit young and impressionable, and angry. God knows why; it's not like I didn't have a fantastic upbringing. I was just a teenager I guess. I got caught up in the wrong crowd, as they say."

"And what, precisely, did you do?"

"Shall I tell you..? Oh go on then. It's a bit embarrassing really. I was arrested for criminal damage to a police van."

"Bloody hell, Jamie! That doesn't sound like you. You must have been *really* angry."

"Well actually, I thought I was being funny. I was showing off, I guess. I spray painted 'How am I driving? Dial 999' on the back of the van."

Simon splutters and then I am laughing too. It was pretty funny, come to think of it. It was just that getting arrested kind of took the edge of it.

I look at him, and we hold each other's gaze for a short moment before looking away again and both calling the collies at the same time. We laugh again and Simon gives me Ruby's lead as the dogs come bowling towards us. I fasten it to her collar and he does the same with Bella, then I put my trainers back on and we walk up into the town, heading for the harbour.

We eat our chips quietly, making sure we sit with our backs against the wall so no scavenging seagulls can sneak up on us from behind.

"Remember Madeleine?" I ask Simon.

"Madeleine? As if I could forget!"

"She's apparently landed a trainee job at one of the nationals," I tell him, "I'm not sure which one."

"Ah well, let's hope it's the *Daily Mail*. She's as full of shit as they are."

I smile at him.

"I had a go at her and Dave that night you know, but they just laughed in my face."

"Really?" I say, wondering why he didn't tell me at the time.

"I didn't know whether to say anything, Jamie. That night was a nightmare from start to finish wasn't it? And I didn't know if it was any of my business. I just felt sure you'd see Dave for the arse that he was and kick him into touch."

"Seems you have a better opinion of me than I deserve," I tell him.

"What, because he left you before you had a chance to tell him to? You would have done it Jamie, eventually. It's hard to see through people sometimes, especially when you're that close to them."

I sit thinking about this, watching the little sparrow which is hopping around hopefully near our feet. The two dogs are lying down next to each other, panting. Heads resting on paws, eyes never quite leaving the chips in Simon's hands.

"Thank you," I tell him, "One of the worst things about what happened is the embarrassment. Of having been so stupid to let him into my life like that. What was I thinking?"

"Well, I knew he was an arse but even I wouldn't have thought he'd have pulled a stunt like he did. God, it's unbelievable. I get angry thinking about it. And I know Russell wants to batter him."

I think, how nice of Simon to be angry on my behalf.

"Do you know what, Simon? You're not too bad, for a farmer."

He nudges me in the rib and, as I nudge him back, he drops the remainder of the chips on the floor. Quick as a flash, the dogs are on their feet, hoovering the chips up with their mouths, not even seeming to bother to chew, while the sparrow hops around at a little distance, not wanting to be left out. I laugh at the dogs. I can't say how good it feels to have made my apology at long last, and together we sit in silence, just watching the boats rocking hypnotically on the gentle harbour waves.

On this sunny blue-skied day, with the dogs at our feet and our cups of tea in hand, I sigh gently as I lean into Simon just a little, testing out this closeness.

Aware that, to passers-by, as we sit here together sipping our cups of tea, we look for all the world like tourists here in this town where we live. Like just any other happy couple.

Congratulations All Round!

Avalon Group are delighted to announce that details of the new structure for *South West News*, our new news service for Devon and Cornwall, have been finalised.

We are especially pleased to confirm that there has been no need for compulsory redundancies, and that all staff from the *Advertiser* will be retaining positions with us.

Congratulations in particular go to Jamie Calder, who will be Deputy Editor – Cornwall Region.

We would also like to welcome on board Dan Fogarty as a full-time photographer.

Although the Head Office is in Exeter, a further satellite office will be located in Penzance and all journalists will be field-based.

Full training will be given to provide all our staff with the skills required to take South West News into the 21st century, creating a fully online and interactive news service.

We will be introducing exciting new schemes which will enable our readers to get personally involved; submitting mobile phone photos and films relating to local stories, making sure that South West News covers every story going and that is truly your news service.

Finally, congratulations must go to Avalon Group Director Jim McKay and his partner Mel, who became proud parents of a beautiful baby girl last month. Mother and baby are doing very well.

Acknowledgements

I owe my thanks to many friends and family who have read *Writing the Town Read* in full or in part, throughout all the different drafts and edits. I am reluctant to name names as I know I will forget someone so I'm taking the cowardly route and just saying thank you to you all, you know who you are!

Special thanks to my parents, Ted and Rosemary Rogers, who have read different versions in full at least a couple of times and have provided much helpful feedback and encouragement.

Thanks also to fellow Heddon authors, Michael Clutterbuck and Peter Clutterbuck, who have been a great source of support and motivation.

To Catherine Clarke – a new friend, keep fit buddy and illustrator, rolled into one - an enormous THANK YOU for my beautiful new cover.

And then of course, there are Chris, Laura and Edward. My husband, daughter and son, who between them all have provided me with support, enthusiasm, and the best reasons possible to stay positive and motivated.

Thank you all x

If you have enjoyed this book, we would be very grateful if you would take the time to review it on the Amazon website. A positive review is invaluable and will be greatly appreciated by the author.

Please also visit the Heddon Publishing website to find out about our other titles: www.heddonpublishing.com

Heddon Publishing was established in 2012 and is a publishing house with a difference. We work with independent authors to get their work out into the real world, by-passing the traditional slog through 'slush piles'.

Please contact us by email in the first instance to find out more:

enquiries@heddonpublishing.com

Like us on Facebook and receive all our news at:

www.facebook.com/heddonpublishing

Join our mailing list by emailing:

mailinglist@heddonpublishing.com

Follow us on Twitter: @PublishHeddon

Printed in Great Britain
by Amazon

44506188R00125